TROUBLE IN THE TREASURE

A NORA JONES MYSTERY

HEATHER HUFFMAN

Copyright 2021 Heather Huffman

This work is licensed under a Creative Commons Attribution-Noncommercial-No Derivative Works 3.0 Unported License.

Attribution — You must attribute the work in the manner specified by the author or licensor (but not in any way that suggests that they endorse you or your use of the work).

Noncommercial — You may not use this work for commercial purposes.

No Derivative Works — You may not alter, transform, or build upon this work.

Cover Design by Madhat Studios

This is a work of fiction. Names, characters, places, brands, media, and incidents are either the product of the author's imagination or are used fictitiously. Any resemblance to similarly named places or to persons living or deceased is unintentional.

For Dylan, my favorite pirate.

I'm not sure there are words to adequately express how much I love and admire you.
Watching your adventure unfold has been, and continues to be, one of my greatest joys.

I will love you always.

CHAPTER ONE

NORA'S EYES ADJUSTED TO THE SUN. SHE WATCHED MARGO CURL and unfurl, the fluid motion lifting the animal off the ground and propelling her body forward. It had been just three short months since Nora had wrapped up her life in San Francisco and officially become a citizen of sunny St. Augustine. Three months, and yet she couldn't quite imagine living anywhere else. It felt like this had always been home.

Granted, it had been a busy three months—full of a thriving business, a friend's art show, and another friend getting his own television show. The days had passed in such a blur she was only just now making good on her promise to her dog that they would go to an off-leash park. Fenced, naturally, because Nora didn't trust the hound not to run all the way to Georgia if she caught sight of something interesting.

Nora swore she could see Margo smiling as she raced by in a blur. She settled herself at a nearby picnic table, content to let the greyhound run as long as she liked. A couple of laps around the perimeter and she was done, panting at Nora's feet, a big old doggie grin on her face as she watched a pair of Goldendoodles play hide and seek in a tunnel.

"You can go make friends, you know." Nora scratched the

dog's ears affectionately. She hadn't wanted a pet of any sort when she inherited Margo along with the bookstore and all the rest of her uncle's considerable assets. Still, the animal had quickly grown on her, and now the two of them were inseparable.

Her phone vibrated and Nora glanced at it. It was a text from her chief mate, Oliver Wessex. The young man had been a sailor on board her salvage vessel, but Nora had seen his potential and quickly promoted him. He wasn't quite ready to be a captain, but he was helping her find a new one she could trust since the previous captain was currently serving a year in county for breaking and entering. Considering it was her home and bookshop he'd broken into, Nora couldn't help feeling a year wasn't quite long enough.

She was in the middle of replying to Oliver her reassurance that she would be there for the interview with the newest candidate when the doodles shifted their attention from the doggie agility course to Margo. The dog, in all her awkward glory, pulled her lips back into an expression Nora now understood to be a smile.

The enthusiastic pups were unfazed by Margo's efforts to placate them, instead bouncing around her with an energy Nora envied. Margo, however, didn't know how to handle the exuberance and inched closer to Nora for protection.

"Lucy, Ethel—come." An Adonis of a man called, striding across the park to reclaim his charges when they cheerfully ignored him.

Nora pressed her lips together in an attempt to curtail her amusement. The man was bronze from head to toe, his hair and skin both kissed by the sun. As he drew nearer, she realized his eyes were shockingly blue, defying the monochromatic theme the rest of him had going. Those pretty blue eyes were crinkled at the corners, though she couldn't say if it was from years of laughter or from squinting against the sun. He wore a button-down shirt with the sleeves rolled up and a pair of cargo shorts.

She wouldn't have been human if she hadn't at least noticed that he had nice muscles.

The incongruence of this man, so favored by the gods, and yet so thoroughly ignored by a pair of Goldendoodles named Lucy and Ethel, was almost too much for Nora.

"They're my sister's," he explained, most likely noting the amusement on her face.

"Ah," she said. As much as Nora hated to be pushy, he was clearly in over his head and Margo had just about hit her wall with the attention she was getting from the pair, so Nora affixed them with her sternest glare, and in a voice that left no room for debate, she quietly commanded, "Lucy, Ethel—sit."

The pair immediately stopped their onslaught and sat, looking to Nora for approval, which she gave in the form of a single nod.

"That was impressive. Are you looking for a job? I might have to hire you as my first mate," he teased.

Nora let it go that she already had a job—two steps above first mate—and asked, "You captain a boat, then?"

He nodded. "A pirate ship, no less."

"Nice. You're not at all what I'd expect from a pirate, but I guess even buccaneers have to change with the times."

He chuckled at that. "Don't worry, when I sail, I look much more pirate-y."

"Pirate-y? Is that a word?"

"Worked well enough just now." He shrugged.

She had to give him that one. "I suppose it did."

"Anyway, thanks for corralling these two monsters for me." He snapped a leash on each dog. "I'm running late for a job interview, thanks to them."

"So, pirates not only wear cargo shorts these days, but they also go on job interviews as well?"

"Job interviews to hunt for treasure," he confirmed. "Times have most definitely changed."

With his statement, the lightbulb clicked on in Nora's brain and she realized sometimes the world can be truly small. "I don't suppose your name is Gregory, is it?"

"Gregory Angelou, why?"

"I'm Nora Jones. I own Mercury Enterprises. The *Amelia* is my boat."

A few expressions crossed his face as he tried to process what she'd just told him. "Well then, when you interview me in an hour, please try to forget that I can't control my sister's dogs."

"Done," she lied. It was going to be difficult to get that image out of her head.

"And I'm sorry about offering you a job as first mate."

"No worries. But you should know the *Amelia* already has a chief mate, and he's quite good. You'll like him."

"Oliver? Yeah, he seems like a good sort."

"He is." Nora smiled. She was proud of how well Oliver had stepped up when given the opportunity. "You should probably go, though, or we'll both be late."

It was hard to say, but Gregory appeared a bit sheepish as he made his exit. Nora looked down at Margo. "One last lap before we leave?"

Margo rested her head on Nora's knee, which she took to mean, "Nope, I'd like my bed now, thanks."

The pair loaded up in the car. Once she was on the road, Nora called to find out what everyone at the shop wanted for breakfast and asked her office manager, Prudence, to order it for them since she was already running late.

"You want me to give the new place next door a try?" Pru asked, the hesitation in her voice evident.

"There's a new place next door?" Nora wasn't sure how she felt about that. Maybe a change of ownership would help her put everything behind her. It hadn't been easy walking past that empty smoothie shop every day, knowing the former owner had murdered her uncle. Still, the place was literally next door to her own bookshop, so it was kind of hard to avoid.

"Yeah, the sign just went up today, but it says they're open for business."

"That feels like poor planning." Nora frowned, thinking she would have put a "coming soon" sign up months ago, had it been her business.

"Aren't you going to ask me what it is?"

Nora could tell by the tone of Pru's voice that she desperately wanted to be asked what kind of business it was.

"What kind of business is it?" She obliged, bracing herself for something like an adult toy store or one of those shops that sold soaps and lotions—Nora had always thought the smell from those things was overwhelming. She wasn't sure she could walk by one every day. If that was their new neighbor, she might have to take to working remotely. But then, if it was either of those shops, Pru wouldn't have suggested it for breakfast, so Nora supposed she was in the clear.

"It's a smoothie shop."

Of all the things Nora thought it could possibly be, that one had not crossed her mind.

"Oh. Um… that feels awfully brave."

"Right? You have to wonder if the new owner knows what went down."

"How could they not know? Regina poisoning Walter was all over the news. I'm fairly certain it's at least partly responsible for our boon in business."

"Hey." As the person in charge of marketing, Pru took exception to that comment.

"I only said partly responsible," Nora clarified. "Obviously your marketing prowess is mostly responsible."

"Now I just feel patronized."

"So, breakfast." Nora changed the subject. "You choose. No smoothies."

Nora smiled as she hung up the phone. Pru had come a long way since they'd first met, back when the bookstore sat empty because Nora's uncle had been trying to give Pru a quiet oasis.

Nora had never even heard of chromesthesia before meeting Prudence, but she'd learned a lot about it since. The condition meant that a visual display accompanied every sound she heard. Something that was stunning painted—as evidenced by the turnout at Pru's first art showing—but was often overwhelming to experience.

While Nora applauded the intent behind Walter's efforts on his employee's behalf, she was far too pragmatic to allow the bookshop to keep losing money hand over fist. Instead, she promoted Prudence to manager, gave her a soundproof office, and charged her with the task of getting them in the black again. Prudence had done splendidly, and Worth Their Salt Books was now a bustling little shop in historic St. Augustine.

As Nora entered said shop, greeted by a bohemian redhead in harem pants and a t-shirt that said, "Not slim, kinda shady," she couldn't help wondering if that success was in spite of the shop's quirky staff, or if they added to the appeal.

They certainly brightened Nora's day, if nothing else.

"Hey, August. Where's Charlotte?" Nora asked, looking around expectantly for the other woman's daughter even as she bent to unhook Margo's leash. The child was usually the first to greet her each morning. Even Margo seemed to miss her, sniffing around the children's reading nook before sighing and trotting back to the office and her bed.

"It's her first day of preschool," August answered. "And I miss the little squirt already."

"Oh, right." Nora tried to hide her disappointment. "I'd forgotten that. It's probably best, though. I mean, just being around adults has to be boring for her."

"She loved it," August assured her. "She was a little put out that I made her go to 'baby school,' as she put it. But she starts kindergarten next year. I thought it might be a good idea for her to ease into being a normal kid."

"Charlotte will never be a normal kid," Nora corrected. "She's much too extraordinary for that."

August beamed in response. Nora didn't know much about the duo's life before their paths crossed with hers, but she suspected it was not an easy one. Something had turned them into nomads. Maybe it had been itchy feet, but there was a shadow in August's eyes that said there was more to the story.

Still, August had been a good mom to Charlotte, turning their flowered van into a cozy little home for the pair as they crisscrossed the country. When August had accepted the job Nora offered her, it had been with the warning that she could pick up and leave at any time—she and Charlotte never stayed in one place long. That was four months ago, and now Charlotte was registered in preschool using Nora's address. She suspected the pair was sticking around a little longer, at least.

The bell above the door tinkled merrily, and they were joined by Leo, who in all likelihood was the real reason August lingered in St. Augustine.

"Did you guys see what went in next door?" he asked without preamble.

Nora sighed heavily. "Yes. I'm not sure how I feel about it."

"I think it's kind of brilliant," August said. "People are pretty twisted. I bet she gets a lot of business just because of the connection."

"Should we go say hi?" Nora fretted. She had no desire to step inside that shop ever again.

"Don't bother." Pru popped her head out of the office. "She'll be over in a few minutes with our breakfast. I offered to come get it, but she said she wanted to come and meet everyone."

Nora must not have done a good job of hiding her irritation because Pru shrugged defensively.

"You said no smoothies, so I ordered us some bakery-type stuff. She has a bacon and spinach quiche that literally made my mouth water even thinking about it."

August and Leo exchanged a look. Nora hated how in sync they were. Well, she didn't hate it, she thought it was adorable, but she hated it because she missed having someone that she could communicate with through just a look. Unbidden, the detective who worked on her uncle's case flitted through her mind. She quickly shoved him right out the door, reminding herself that she and Detective Medero—Rafael—had forged a nice little friendship and that's how she wanted it to stay.

There was no time to debate the issue because their new neighbor was backing through the door, her arms laden with boxes of goodies for them. Leo scrambled to help even as Nora plastered a smile on her face and greeted her with a warm hello.

"Hi, I'm Mykal." Her smile was lovely, though shy. The woman was tiny, maybe five feet tall if she stretched herself. She had long, mahogany hair that tumbled down her back, the last few inches of it dyed a deep red that was almost maroon. She had dark eyes, long lashes, and a heart-shaped face.

"It's nice to meet you Mykal." August came out from around the counter to take one of the boxes from her. "I'm August. The one that looks like she stepped out of the 1940s over there is Nora. The pixie with blue hair is Pru. And that adorable man is Leo."

Nora tilted her head and looked at August, not sure whether to be offended or laugh at her frank descriptions of all of them.

"Pixie with blue hair?" Pru raised her eyebrows. "Blue streaks, thank you very much. The rest is blonde."

"That's what you chose to argue?" Leo questioned.

Pru shrugged. "I don't know. It seemed pretty spot-on."

"It was nice of you to bring everything over." Nora changed the subject. "Pru is pretty excited about the quiche."

"I just wanted to say hi and maybe get the awkward first meeting out of the way," Mykal explained. "I can only imagine how you must feel about me and the shop. I hope we can be friends, though."

"It will take some getting used to," Nora admitted. "But we always knew the place wouldn't sit empty forever."

"I have to say we weren't expecting another smoothie shop,"

Leo interjected. He had a way of being so friendly in his brutal honesty that it never came off as rude.

"It's a bakery, too." Mykal illustrated the point by opening one of the boxes August had set on the counter. "To be honest, my partner insisted on the smoothies. She said it would bring in the curious and a new business needs all the help it can get."

"Ha!" August was oddly triumphant. "I told you it was a brilliant business strategy."

Nora smiled and let the conversation roll around her. She didn't begrudge her new neighbors opening a shop or even using whatever tools they had at their disposal to increase foot traffic. Still, it brought a twinge of pain with it. Moreover, there was something about the shop's new owner that didn't sit well with her. She couldn't put her finger on it, but she felt like she'd seen her before.

CHAPTER TWO

SHE WAS GLAD FOR THE DISTRACTION WHEN OLIVER SHOWED UP JUST moments before Gregory Angelou arrived for his interview.

Oliver's dreadlocks had grown out a bit in the time since they'd known each other. She noticed he'd taken to dressing sharper since his promotion. He was a smart man who wasn't about to squander the opportunity he'd been given, so he took his role seriously. However unimpressive Gregory might have been at the dog park, if Oliver wanted him as the Amelia's captain, Nora would trust him.

Oliver greeted her with his typical easy grin and a warm hug. Their hellos were cut short when he spotted the baked goods sprawled across the counter. Much to Pru's relief, he bypassed the quiche and headed straight for the blueberry lemon muffins. His cheeks were loaded up like a squirrel's when Gregory arrived for his interview, taking in the scene before him with a certain measure of skepticism.

Margo, lured by the smell of food and the sound of so many voices, had appeared from the office and now sat staring attentively at the counter, wagging her tail and giving her most beseeching look to anyone who made the mistake of glancing her direction. Leo, August, and Pru were chatting animatedly with Mykal, plotting out all the ways that the two businesses could cross-promote each other in the coming months.

"As you can see, Captain Angelou, I run a tight ship around here," Nora quipped. As if to illustrate her point, a muffin rolled off the counter, sending Margo skittering after it.

"Yes, I can see that. You're quite the taskmaster."

"Would you like some quiche before we get started?" she offered. "It appears Oliver and Margo have made short work of the muffins."

"I'm good, thanks."

Nora nodded, then turned her attention to Pru. "We're going to snag the office for a bit."

Pru seemed unconcerned, so Nora led the two men back to the shop's lone office. It occurred to her that she might want to see about leasing an office space of her own, a place she could manage the other businesses from. She also wondered if she could entice Ivy, her part-time accountant, to come work for her full-time. She'd inherited more than one business from her uncle. It had taken Nora and Ivy months to sort out the man's jumbled books—recordkeeping had not been Walter's forte—but they were starting to get a sense of what was what, and both women had ideas about how to grow and reshape Mercury Enterprises into a business that could withstand the changing economic landscape.

Grow it, shape it, and cut the company's loose ties with the mafia.

Nora didn't have time to dwell on that now, as they seated themselves around the desk. As she'd done so many times throughout her career, Nora settled easily into the power seat and leaned back, keeping her body language open and confident as she smiled at Gregory Angelou and began the interview.

She listened as he recounted the milestones of his career, his journey from deckhand up through the ranks to captain. She got the sense he was bored at his current job, but he'd skirted around why he'd left a lucrative gig captaining a major cargo ship to shuttle tourists around in a recreated pirate ship. In fact, the one thing that jumped out at Nora as he spoke was the depth of this man's experience. He'd had a lot of jobs for someone who couldn't be more than forty.

"I'm impressed with the range of experience," Nora began, pausing to think through her next words. "Can you walk me through why there is so much variety on your resume?"

Gregory grinned, reminding her once more how disarmingly handsome he was. "Why am I such a job hopper, you mean?"

Oliver looked like he wanted to jump to the other man's defense, but it wasn't necessary. Gregory spoke with the confidence of someone certain of their choices.

"It's not uncommon for sailors to be drifters to some degree. Still, I would love to find a career home. To captain a ship for the long-term. But I won't be silent if I see the company I work for doing something wrong. I have a responsibility to my crew and to the ocean—if you jeopardize either, I will speak up."

"So, you're saying you've been let go from your previous positions because of your scruples?"

"Scruples." He chuckled. "There's a word you don't hear often anymore."

Nora waited, watching him, unafraid of the silence. She'd found it was often the best tool for getting others to talk.

"Yes, ma'am. Dumping illegal toxic waste, overloading the ship, failing to reinforce the hull… If you'd like, I can walk you through each company. I remember them well."

"That won't be necessary." Nora shook her head. "I believe I've heard enough. Thank you so much for your time today. We'll be in touch."

Nora rose, shaking his hand before Oliver led him back to the front. She waited in the office for the younger man to return, mulling over Captain Angelou's words as she did.

Oliver returned, looking almost like a dejected puppy. "I know you didn't like him, but for once I have to disagree with you, Nora. You won't find a better captain than Gregory Angelou."

"Didn't like him?" Nora furrowed her brow. "Quite the contrary, I happen to think he's exactly what we need. I just don't want to offer him the position until I see him at work."

"Oh." Nora's response took the wind out of Oliver's sails. "You liked him?"

"Very much."

"You didn't seem especially friendly."

"Was I rude?" Nora had been told by more than one man that she could come across as cold. She never intended to be, sometimes she just got wrapped up in her thoughts and forgot to regulate her face.

"Not rude," Oliver assured her. "Just not warm."

"Hmm." Nora let it go at that, wondering if her gender played a role in the expectation of warmth. She suspected it was more likely that her gender played a role in people feeling comfortable mentioning it. "I'd like you to please keep our conversation between us. I'm not prepared to go on record with my thoughts until I've done a little digging of my own."

Oliver happily agreed, relieved that he'd most likely be getting to work with the captain he seemed to almost hero worship. Nora wasn't left alone with her thoughts for long before Prudence slid into the office, eager for some quiet and a break from the veritable rainbow of sound in the shop this morning.

Nora snagged her laptop off the desk and went in search of a corner of the store where she could work. The place was oddly packed for a weekday in the middle of winter, but then Nora realized it was a filming day, and people were filtering in hoping to catch a glimpse of whoever Leo had brought in for this week's celebrity guest.

When she'd met Leo, he'd been a one-man show, in town to film an episode of his fairly unknown YouTube show *Ghosthunters, Inc*. But it turned out one of the other hotel guests was a fairly well-known actress and socialite, and he'd charmed her into being a guest on the show as a lark, interviewing her about the unexplained phenomena she'd encountered while staying at the inn widely believed to be haunted.

The episode had gone viral, and the whole thing snowballed until Leo found himself with a contract for a reality TV show chasing stories of ghosts and cryptids around the country, often with the help of random celebrities and pseudo-celebrities. Although, upon thinking about it, Nora questioned the validity of calling something like that "reality" TV. And, in truth, she had her doubts about Casimir Whitlock, the producer who'd shown up out of the blue offering Leo a television deal. The man was entirely too slick for Nora's liking.

It was all fairly new, and Leo had thus far been able to keep their locations suspiciously close to St. Augustine. But his producer was insistent he branch out, so Leo would be leaving them soon to spend six weeks chasing a sasquatch in Maine, an evil spirit in Rhode Island, and looking into the Croatoan legend of North Carolina. Nora had no doubt that if it wasn't for Charlotte, August would be packing her bags for Maine right now. Which told Nora it was true love because she imagined Maine was pretty danged cold and snowy at the moment. Not that either of them would admit it. The part about it being love; she was certain they had no qualms admitting Maine was cold.

For a second time that morning, Rafael crept into her thoughts. This time he wasn't so easily shoved aside because he was texting, asking her if she wanted to go to dinner. Unfortunately—or fortunately, depending on how she looked at it—she already had plans for her evening. So, she made plans to meet Rafael at Meehan's patio the next evening before turning her attention to cyberstalking Gregory Angelou and the companies he'd previously worked for.

She got so engrossed in that, she almost made herself late for dinner. When she noticed the time, she let out a soft expletive and hurried home to get ready, wondering what exactly one wore to eat dinner on a pirate ship.

CHAPTER THREE

"Tell me again why we are having drinks on the biggest tourist trap in town?" Ivy glanced about the boat with disdain.

Nora smirked, unwilling to take the bait. "I didn't tell you the first time. Now loosen up and at least pretend to have fun. You know, life only loses its magic if you let it."

"You've been spending too much time hanging out in your uncle Walter's world. That sounds like something he would have said."

Nora took that as a compliment, warming inside at the thought of the uncle she'd come to love so dearly after his death. She'd never known him in life, but she was certain they would have gotten along.

The women sat at a table tucked up in a corner, close to the railing. The whole thing might be a tourist trap, but Nora was still enchanted by it: the roll of the sea, the slap of the waves at the ship, the mist in the air. All of it. She wondered if there were any whales in this part of the ocean this time of year and if they might see one.

"I could get addicted to this," she said.

"Oh no." Ivy shook her head. "I don't know how you got me

on this boat the first time. We will not be eating dinner at sea a second time. I got sauce on my favorite blouse. Nuh-uh."

"That was unfortunate." Nora sobered briefly. It had been a cute blouse and it was most definitely ruined. "But I was referring to being at sea in general. I get why Walter loved it so much. And I'll replace the blouse. I am sorry about that."

"Don't worry about the blouse." Ivy softened. "But I still don't understand—"

Her words were cut short when Nora shrank back into the shadows, trying to avoid being seen. Ivy glanced about, trying to find what her friend was hiding from when her gaze landed on a tall, bronzed pirate walking from table to table, greeting guests.

"Oh, Oh, my. That is one fine-looking man. He can pillage me any day."

"Ivy." Nora couldn't help giggling, taking the sting out of her admonishment.

"He's why we're here, isn't he? What happened to Detective Mc-Cutey-butt?"

"It's not like that. And I've told you Detective Medero and I are just friends."

"Every woman in town wants to eat that man for dessert and *you* put *him* in the friend zone? You are crazy, Nora Jones."

"Nora Jones?" The pirate in question stood at their table, looking down at Nora with curiosity written plainly on his face. "Are you checking up on me?"

"I am." She saw no sense in trying to hide it now. "I was hoping to see you in action without being caught, but it seems I'm a bit rusty at being stealthy."

"I didn't expect to hear from you again," he admitted. "Except for maybe a 'thanks but no thanks' email."

Ivy cleared her throat before Nora could answer, wanting an introduction.

"Captain Angelou, this is my friend Ivy Clarke. Ivy, this is Gregory Angelou. Hopefully, he's the next captain of the *Amelia*."

Gregory's grin was instant and genuine. "Yeah?"

Nora matched his smile. "Absolutely. We can talk details tomorrow, but *Amelia* needs a captain not afraid to do what's right, even if it's not easy."

"Right is seldom easy."

"Too true," Nora agreed.

"Congratulations, Captain Angelou." Ivy practically batted her eyelashes at the man.

"Thank you." He turned his attention to her. "It was a pleasure to meet you."

"Ivy is the one who makes sure we all get paid, so I'm sure you'll see her again."

"Ah, the woman with the money, then it really is a pleasure to meet you." He winked playfully and Ivy darn near melted right there on the spot.

She watched him leave, not noticing right away that Nora was openly watching her, eyebrows raised and barely winning the battle with her grin.

"Don't you judge me." Ivy grew defensive once she did notice her friend's expression. "That is a fine, fine man."

"He is."

"And you have Detective Mc-Cutey-butt."

Nora rolled her eyes, not even bothering to protest since it was clearly falling on deaf ears.

"I have sauce on my shirt." Ivy's face contorted in horror. "I just met a Greek god in the flesh, and I have sauce—On. My. Shirt." She punctuated each word, lest Nora miss the gravity of the situation.

"It's hardly even noticeable."

"You are a terrible liar."

Nora knew her friend wasn't wrong—the sauce stain was super noticeable, and Nora was a terrible liar—so rather than argue with facts, she changed the subject. "Captain Dreamy isn't the only reason I asked you to meet me for dinner tonight."

TROUBLE IN THE TREASURE

"You mean, there's more to this evening? Because I don't know if my heart can take another one of those."

"Not another man." Nora was genuinely amused by Ivy's reaction to Gregory. She'd hoped they'd like each other, but Ivy's response was so uncharacteristically over the top, Nora would be mentally giggling about this for a while. "I was actually wondering how you'd feel about being my CFO."

Ivy laughed, sobering when she realized Nora wasn't laughing with her. "Oh. You're serious."

"My uncle and I might be alike in many ways, but we differ in this: I know when I'm in over my head and I'm not willing to risk all he built—all we've built—to chance. I'm all for appreciating that life is a grand adventure, but I don't think we have to throw practicality out the window."

"I'm listening." Ivy carefully stacked their plates and set them aside, leaning forward to better hear what Nora had to say.

Nora leaned in as well and spent the remainder of the evening with the thrill of sea forgotten as she told Ivy her plans for Mercury Enterprises and the rest of her uncle's holdings, which she was slowly beginning to fully comprehend were her holdings.

In the spirit of beginning to claim this world as her own—and stop acting like she was merely a guest in it—that night, after she'd changed into her pajamas and walked Margo, she took a deep breath and grabbed a box.

She'd spent the past couple of months slowly sorting through and packing up the belongings in Walter's bedroom, starting with the master bath, then moving to the closet, inching her way through his most private spaces. Some things, she'd kept. Some, she'd given to his friends or to Raymond, the man who'd been Walter's partner through life. She'd donated a fair share of his belongings. And now, it was time to go through her uncle's nightstand. Then the room would be empty. In theory, ready for her to move out of the guest room. She wasn't sure she was ready for that, but at least this task would be done.

Nora certainly wasn't ready for what she found when she opened the drawer. At first, it yielded the usual contents: a book, a heating pad, a bottle of pain reliever. Nora held up the flask and grinned. "Uncle Walter, you scamp."

But sitting at the bottom, just waiting to be found, was a manila envelope with her name scrawled on it. She carefully emptied the contents on the ground. There was what looked to be a super old piece of paper, folded up and sealed in a plastic bag. But Nora only had eyes for the note that came with it.

My dearest Nora,

If you are reading this, it means you've finally gotten around to cleaning out my nightstand. If you're anything like me, it took you a while to work up to it. I want you to know that it was never my intent to hurt your mother or leave my family behind, but their world was a cage I could no longer abide, and sometimes you just have to choose yourself. Perhaps it was selfish of me. I deeply regret not being part of your life, my dear.

Still, my life has been an adventure, full of friendship and love. I wish that for you, too, Nora. It's my hope that by leaving my world in your care, I've given you that. I cannot make up for being absent so much of your life, but perhaps this is a start.

My doctor tells me I am imagining it, but I know I am dying. I can feel it deep in my bones that something's not right. I hope you're not cross with me, but I've given the Magnolia Jane to dear Lucca. That boat kept me grounded to the dreams of my youth, kept me from getting too jaded. I hope she does the same for him. I worry about my friend after I'm gone. His world pulls him to dark places.

But everything else, I have left to you. My sweet Margo is most prized of all I have to give. Second to her is this map. It was to be my grandest adventure yet, but it was not meant to be.

When I first bought the Amelia and Lucca and I set out, it was a lark. A grown man living his childhood pirate dreams. We followed in the footsteps of the greats, learned the ropes from those who'd discovered some of the biggest treasure hauls of our age.

But lately, something doesn't feel right. Maybe I'm just getting old, but I worry about the damage the big boats cause. I wonder if our finds belong in a museum and not a vault. And I suspect someone is using my boat, using me, to do bad things. I wish I could tell you more, but much like my suspicions about my health, I only have a feeling in my gut that something's amiss.

So, take this map, dear one, and use it to go on your own pirate adventure. If you're not sure where to start, talk to Arin Lancaster over at the lighthouse. They're a friend who'll steer you straight. But be careful who you trust. There is an old saying that rings true: Where there's treasure, there's trouble.

Love always,
Walter

Nora rocked back, absorbing what she'd read. He'd known he was dying, and nobody had believed him. There was a lot to unpack in his note, but that part of it was breaking her heart. She wondered if Raymond knew about the letter. Had he known Walter was concerned about his health? Surely not. Nora caught a cold and the man had pestered her for a week solid to get it checked out. If he'd suspected Walter was ill, he would have hounded the doctors until they'd found the solution.

Some part of her wanted to share the note with Raymond, to find out if he knew about the treasure. But the larger part of her wasn't ready to share it with anyone just yet. Almost as an afterthought, she carefully slid the map out of its wrapping and unfolded it, laying it gently on the floor.

"Huh. It's an honest-to-God treasure map." Nora wasn't sure what she'd expected, but it still seemed weird that it actually looked like a treasure map should look. She thought that was an "only in movies" kind of thing.

She carefully folded the map and note back up, sliding them into their envelope and taking them with her to her bedroom and placing it in the top drawer of her own nightstand. Sleep eluded her for much of the night. She kept thinking about the map and what it might lead to.

When the first rays of sunlight trickled through her window, she gave up on sleep and went through the motions of her morning routine. Margo bounded around her feet happily, completely oblivious to the fact that Nora felt like the walking dead.

Once she'd dressed in her snappy grey slacks and a coral blouse with the cutest little ruffles, she tucked the envelope in her purse, rounded up Margo, and headed out the door, but not before texting Raymond to see if he was game to meet her for breakfast.

They met at her favorite spot, a hole-in-the-wall downtown diner that served classic breakfast fare and didn't complain when she brought Margo along, which was always. Nora waited until they were settled before broaching the reason she'd wanted to meet. She'd debated whether or not to even show him the note, not sure if it would only cause pain at this point. Ultimately, she'd decided that if it had been her partner, she'd want to know.

With that in mind, she slid the envelope across the table at him. "I found this last night."

Confusion darted across his face as he carefully slid the contents out on the table. First reading the note, as Nora had done, and then gingerly examining the map. "Well, my dear, it seems you've inherited a proper adventure."

"Every day has been an adventure since the moment you called me, Raymond."

He chuckled at that. "You are not wrong."

"But a treasure map? How do I even go about something like this? I wouldn't know where to start."

"You love solving mysteries. If it wasn't for you, I don't know we ever would have known who killed sweet Walter."

"I like solving mysteries that require internet research and talking to people and maybe a bit of snooping around. Tromping through the jungle is not my forte."

"Don't be dramatic. Florida doesn't have jungles."

"You have panthers. And alligators."

"I'd be more concerned about the mosquitos if I were you. They are the size of small birds here."

"You're just making fun of me now."

"I am," he admitted, his chuckle deepening to laughter.

Nora took the map and refolded it, tucking it safely away while she waited for him to get control of himself.

"Oh, my dear. I'm so sorry Walter never got to meet you. He would have been absolutely delighted."

"And I in him," she assured him, knowing how much he missed his dearest friend.

"You have to do this. For him, if not yourself."

"You think?"

"There's a reason he wanted it to be you." Raymond grew serious. "He didn't even tell me about it. That means something."

Nora considered his words. Her life had been entirely upside down since coming to Florida—sometimes in a good way, sometimes not. She'd taken it all in stride, but the thought of wandering the woods with a compass and a map felt a bit excessive.

On the other hand, Walter had done so much for the people in his world, her included, and he'd never asked for a thing in return. If he wanted her to do this one thing, however absurd, she couldn't deny him.

"Okay. I'll do it." Nora took the note from Raymond and looked down at it once more, running her fingers over the words

Walter had scrawled, as if feeling them might somehow tether her to the man.

Margo chuffed under the table, drawing Nora's attention from the note. She looked about to see what Margo was warning her about, her gaze landing on Lucca Buccio, the mob boss who'd been an unlikely friend to her uncle. Even though the man had always been kind to Nora, she instinctively slid the note back in the envelope with the map and tucked both in her purse.

"Ah, it's Nora, Raymond, and Margo. How wonderful." Lucca greeted them warmly with kisses on the cheek all around.

"Lucca, how are you?" Nora settled back into her chair, motioning to an empty chair at the table. "Care to join us?"

"Unfortunately, I'm here on business, but we still need to have that dinner you keep promising me."

"Soon," she promised yet again, thinking Rafael would have an aneurysm if he knew. Oddly, her detective friend wasn't fond of her mafia friend. Nora didn't trust him herself, but he had been good to Walter, and he'd been good to her. If she set aside what he did for a living, he was a perfectly nice man. But that was an awfully big if.

After a few minutes of small talk between the three of them, Lucca moved on, leaving Nora and Ray alone at their table. Still, they didn't circle back to talk of the map. Instead, Raymond filled her in on his secretary, Lissa, and the news of her engagement. They were training a temp to take over while Lissa was on her honeymoon, but it wasn't going well—the temp was more interested in taking selfies than answering the phone.

The whole conversation made Nora even more grateful for her staff at the bookshop. They might be an odd bunch, but they made her smile each and every day. She already thought of them more as family than coworkers.

When breakfast was over, the pair parted ways with a fond hug. Nora headed over to the historic district, intentionally parking well away from the store so she had an excuse to walk off some of the breakfast. She was so full she felt like she could pop.

She noticed him long before she reached him—the handsome detective she was so determined to keep in the friend zone. He was walking out of the bakery (Nora refused to call it a smoothie shop), two coffee cups in hand.

"You're a daring man," Nora observed by way of hello.

"What are the odds it'll be owned by two murderous maniacs in a row, right?"

"I suppose I see the logic."

"That's good because one of these is for you." He held a cup out to her.

She didn't have the heart to tell him she was stuffed to the gills from breakfast. Besides, she was in dire need of caffeine. It was worth making room for. She accepted the cup gratefully, falling in line beside him as they wandered, her path to the bookstore forgotten. They both knew he'd lose her attention once she walked through the doors of the shop, so they held off.

"You look pretty this morning," he commented.

She blushed. "So you do." And he did; he was always impeccably dressed in a perfectly coordinated linen suit. With his thick, black hair, deep brown eyes, caramel skin, and angular features, he was a beautiful man. Add to that the muscles you could see hiding under that suit and it was no wonder he left a trail of broken hearts behind him without even meaning to.

So far, she'd successfully avoided being one of those broken hearts. Having lost her fiancé to an accident years ago, Nora hadn't even considered opening her heart again to another in all this time. Rafael had accepted her decree they would just be friends, even if everyone else thought she was insane for making it.

"You do, however, look tired," he amended his earlier compliment.

"I don't think you're ever supposed to say that to a woman."

"Simply reporting the facts as I see them." He held up his hands to show his innocence.

"Don't make me change my mind about dinner."

"Actually, that's why I'm here. Meehan's is going to be packed tonight."

"Oh, it's okay if you need to cancel." Relief warred with disappointment.

"Not cancel, just move plans," he assured her. "How do you feel about me cooking dinner for us at your place?"

"I am in the mood for steak."

"Steak, huh?" He grinned at her. "What's the occasion?"

"No occasion." She shrugged. "But steak sounds good, and we have lots to talk about."

"We do? Like what?" If there was a glimmer of hope in his voice, Nora chose to ignore it.

She did, however, make the decision to trust him. "To be honest, I'm planning a treasure hunt and I haven't the faintest clue where to start."

CHAPTER FOUR

NOT SURPRISINGLY, RAFAEL HAD ASSUMED SHE WAS JOKING. NORA decided to wait to dispel him of the assumption until dinner that evening.

As expected, her attention had immediately shifted the moment she walked through the door of the shop. She tripped over a pile of books, sending images of shirtless men skittering across the floor. Margo hopped over the melee without missing a beat.

"Oops." August appeared from behind a shelf. "I forgot to move those before we opened."

Nora scooped up a stack of books and set them to the side, where they'd be less likely to be a road hazard. "Why are all the bare-chested man covers at the front of the store?"

"It's Valentine's weekend, silly."

"It's what?" Nora paled. She had totally forgotten the date when she'd agreed to dinner with Rafael.

"You made plans with the detective tonight, didn't you?" August smirked.

"Don't laugh."

"How did you not notice the hearts all over, well, pretty much everywhere?"

"I don't know."

"You can be so observant somedays and then others… not."

"Gee, thanks."

August shrugged. "Just an observation."

"Ha, ha." Nora made a face, noting that August's t-shirt said, "I like romantic walks to the taco truck." Undoubtedly a tip of the hat to the holiday.

"You are not canceling plans on that man," August informed her.

"How do you know I was going to cancel?"

"I know you."

"I'm not canceling," Nora retorted, defensive. She had absolutely planned on canceling, but now she couldn't out of sheer stubbornness. "And isn't it a little late to be setting up our Valentine's display?"

August shrugged. "The idea just came to me last night."

"Fair enough. Do you need help?"

"Nah, I got this."

Nora left August to it and went to check in with Prudence. After reassuring her all was well on her end, Pru asked to take off early so she could meet with Diane Fuller at the art gallery down the street. She'd been invited to have a permanent display there.

"That's amazing news!" Nora gushed.

The other woman seemed almost bashful about it. "Yeah, I'm still processing it all."

"We still need to get you a proper studio."

"I'm okay in the loft." Pru tried to wave her off.

"Nope. I'm not listening to that. I have to take care of a few emails, but then you and I are going real estate hunting."

The tiny blonde made a face at Nora, though it didn't disguise her pleasure at the prospect of having an actual art studio to work in. "You're as stubborn as your uncle. You know that, right?"

"I prefer to think of it as tenacious."

"There's a difference?"

Nora simply shrugged and gathered up her laptop to go find a quiet corner of the shop. If she was being completely honest, she'd admit that part of her desire to get Prudence in an art studio was to free up her loft. Maybe then she could convince Leo to move his equipment up there and she'd get her paranormal section back. Or, better yet, she'd move the paranormal section upstairs with Leo and expand her inventory.

It amused her how Leo had become a permanent fixture in their little group. They'd come a long way since the day he stopped to see if he could help when Margo was showing her tenacious streak, refusing to climb the stairs to Nora's hotel room.

Personally, Nora didn't believe in the paranormal, but she liked Leo. So, when he'd asked about filming his show from her bookshop, which he swore was haunted, she'd agreed. It seemed harmless enough. Only the show had become popular enough to land a television deal, and now a third of her store was overtaken by ghost hunting tech and camera crews.

Nora would be relieved when they took their act on the road. Of course, the flip side of that was going to be August. With her daughter in school and Leo gone, August was going to be a lost puppy. Nora could already see that coming.

Setting aside her musings, Nora opened her laptop and got to work putting together an offer letter and contract for her new captain. After that, she emailed Oliver to let him know they could call off the search. His response was immediate and effusive. She promised to follow up soon to set up time for the three of them to meet.

First, she needed to figure out where that might be. She had no idea how her uncle had managed to run everything from his tiny office in the bookshop. Even if Nora hadn't gifted it to Prudence, it didn't seem possible. Of course, that could also be why his finances were such a jumbled mess. A mess Nora was still determined to untangle.

To that end, she texted Ivy to see if her friend had thought any more about their conversation from the night before.

"It's hard to think about much besides that fine pirate of yours," Ivy replied.

"He's not my pirate."

"But he is fine."

Nora texted back a little eyeroll emoji.

"If I'm going to be your CFO, you can't roll your eyes at me every time I pause to admire Captain Angelou."

"So that's a yes?" Nora typed, quickly followed by, "Don't get me sued for sexual harassment."

Ivy texted back an angel emoji, to which Nora did roll her eyes.

"I need to find an office space for me and a studio for Pru." Nora changed the subject. "Any ideas?"

"What about your commercial property over on King Street?"

"I have a commercial property on King Street?"

"Did you not read the report I sent?"

"I started to."

"Yes, you have a property on King Street. The management company will have the keys if you don't."

"What's the address?"

"Read the report."

Nora huffed and looked over at Margo, muttering, "Well, that was rude."

Margo swiveled her ears in what Nora was sure was agreement.

Nora sighed, pulling up the report Ivy mentioned. She promised herself she'd come back and read the whole thing later. For now, she did a Ctrl+F to find the property in question. She'd remembered Walter buying up properties to stop developers from snapping them up, but she'd thought they were all vacant lots. She hadn't realized she was a landlord.

After rifling through the shelf under the front counter, she turned up a post-it note and jotted down the address for both the property and the company managing it. She glanced at the numbers Ivy had sent and was pleased to know they had at least one business running in the black right now.

That done, she stashed her laptop under the counter and went to round up Pru. It was a short drive to the management office. They seemed surprised to see her but welcomed her warmly regardless. The property was a small retail strip with two vacancies and two tenants who'd just renewed their lease: a tattoo parlor and a donut shop.

They got the keys to the vacant units and headed over. Nora decided she liked the place as soon as she pulled up. The largest store was painted aqua blue. It had three smaller stores attached, each of those with a rock facing. The blue one was empty, so they started there. Nora could tell by the look on Pru's face that she wanted the space but didn't want to be greedy.

"I'm not the expert, but this looks like it would be a perfect art studio," Nora commented as she examined the space.

"I could take the smaller one," Pru offered.

"You could, but I think this one has better light. And it's big enough that you could open your own gallery if you decided to. Nothing fancy, just a small independent thing."

Pru's eyes shone as she looked around. "I know just where I'd put everything."

"Then you should definitely take the space," Nora urged. "We'll have Ivy draw up the paperwork."

"I don't know; I can't afford—"

"The paperwork is a formality." Nora interrupted. "It won't cost you anything. You'll be the first recipient of Mercury Enterprises' Hummingbird Grant."

"What on earth is that?"

"I'm going to use my money to invest in other women," Nora explained. "Ivy is helping me set it up."

Prudence stopped and stared at Nora. "That's amazing. Walter would love it."

Nora blushed, ducking the praise by going to examine a door

that seemed to be hanging slightly crooked. "You're going to want your landlord to take a look at that."

"Very funny."

"Seriously, though. Let me know when you're ready to start moving things in. I'll get Leo and Oliver to help."

"That's big of you." Pru laughed, spinning around in the center of the open space one more time.

Nora allowed Pru a couple more minutes to wander and daydream before moving the party on. The next-door neighbor was the tattoo parlor. Maybe someday she'd work up the nerve enough to get a tattoo. Today was not that day.

The door in between the tattoo shop and the donut shop was hers. Like the tattoo shop, hers had a rock façade and a glass door with a brown frame. She couldn't say why, but the whole building gave her an 80s-tourist town vibe. It pleased her.

She looked it over, making a note in her phone to pick up some paint for the place. The drab brown walls were depressing. Nora wasn't sure what had been here before, but she wasn't surprised it had gone out of business.

After they left, they swung back by the management shop to take care of the paperwork. By the time Nora returned Pru to the bookshop, they were both the proud tenants of a new work space. In all, a good day's effort.

As Nora pulled in her driveway that evening, she noticed a "For Sale" sign had gone up in the yard next door. She hoped that meant she'd be trading up in the neighbor department. She'd be thrilled with someone who was content to wave in passing and ignore each other otherwise.

Of course, when Rafael showed up thirty minutes later, that was the first thing he commented on. "I noticed Tom Chapman put his house up for sale."

"I noticed that as well."

"I wonder if your buddy Lucca chased him off."

"He's not my buddy Lucca, and he only threatened Tom the one time."

"Only the once."

Nora couldn't tell if he was amused or not. "Tom was bullying me."

"Just remember that no matter how much he appears to be, Lucca is not tame." Rafael's voice was gentle, cautious almost. She imagined he was cognizant of not patronizing her, lest she stomp him with her incredibly cute heels. They might have a bow at the ankle, but they were dangerous, nonetheless.

"Duly noted." Nora could understand Rafael's concern, but it still irritated her. "Now, are you going to make me food? Or are you going to continue to lecture me about random acquaintances?"

"I kind of thought I could do both."

"Nice. Very nice."

The playful banter continued as they worked together to make dinner. She'd bought the groceries for filet mignon because it was her favorite and she'd made her strawberry walnut salad because it was his.

When everything was prepared, they sat on her patio sipping a glass of wine and savoring their meal. The lights Nora had hung twinkled merrily. Margo sat at attention, watching every morsel that moved from fork to mouth, just in case someone missed the target and sent steak her direction.

"So, the reason I asked you to dinner tonight—" she began, only to be cut off by Rafael.

"I knew it. I told the guys at the station not to read too much into dinner tonight; you'd forgotten it was Valentine's."

She blinked. "You talk about me with the guys at the station?"

"You don't talk about me at the shop?"

"So, anyway," she redirected the conversation. "The reason I asked you over is I found something, and I need your help figuring out what to do next."

"Oh. Sounds serious. What is it?"

"A treasure map."

"Excuse me?"

"There was a treasure map in Walter's nightstand, along with a note."

"I'm surprised you're not all over a mystery like this."

"I guess I just don't know what to make of it—or where to start," she admitted, handing him the envelope and waiting patiently while he read the note and looked over the map.

"I think I'd start with this Arin Lancaster."

"I called and requested an appointment. It'll be Tuesday before they can meet with me. Do you think this is what James Byrd was looking for when he broke into my house?"

"But why? James was chasing a treasure offshore. This is a land map."

Nora frowned, feeling a bit sheepish. "I don't know. I guess it just feels like a bit of a coincidence. And in three months of looking, I've yet to find anything else that would be worth breaking and entering for—here or at the shop."

"What about Walter's books?"

Nora recalled how certain Rafael had once been that Walter's accounting records would show that his money came from less-than-legitimate sources. She'd thought he'd set that aside, but now she wasn't so sure. "Squeaky clean, officer, I promise."

"I didn't mean to ruin our not-Valentine's dinner." He gave her a repentant look. "Forget I mentioned it."

"He was a good man." Nora wasn't quite willing to let it go.

"I have no doubt he did many good things, among them bringing you to Florida." He artfully avoided agreeing with her. "Will you let me know what you find out about the map on Tuesday?"

"Of course." Nora smiled, allowing the conversation to move on. Still, the tone of the evening had changed and when it was time for the couple to part ways, she wasn't entirely sad to have some time alone.

CHAPTER FIVE

It was only two days, but it felt like an eternity. The map tucked in her purse called to her like a telltale heart, never allowing her to forget its presence. When she wasn't working, she studied it for hours. Nora was certain she'd figured out at least some of the drawings on it—if there wasn't a tree shaped like a snake, she'd be sorely disappointed. There was a body of water with cypress trees at the big red X. Still, she'd yet to find anything indicating where to start, and the clues on the map were worthless without that piece of information. This was Florida, and there was undoubtedly more than one body of water with Cypress trees in it.

There was nothing to do but wait for her meeting with Arin, so she threw herself into work. She'd never painted a wall before, but it turned out hiring a professional painter on a Sunday with no notice was difficult, so she told herself she was a competent woman and made the decision to don a pair of overalls and a ratty t-shirt to just do it herself. As she piled her hair on top of her head in a messy bun, she was almost glad to be tackling this project alone. Nora's mother was in Napa, California right now and Nora could still feel the disdain for her state of disarray reaching out across the miles.

By lunchtime, she had more paint on herself and the ceiling than she did the walls—Margo was even sporting coastal blue streaks down each side. At least the smell of freshly baked donuts from next door had abated, or maybe it had just been covered up by paint fumes. She'd have to buy an entirely different wardrobe if she made stopping by there a habit. Still, her stomach rumbled, reminding her that she'd have to take a break to get food from somewhere.

"Whatdya' say, Margo, shall we find some lunch?" Nora squatted to scratch the dog's ears as she spoke. Margo responded by giving Nora a kiss on the nose.

The dog stayed glued to her side as Nora covered the paint cans and wrapped her brushes to keep them from drying out, making the whole process more awkward than it needed to be. That taken care of, she washed up and ran to grab herself lunch at a funky little food truck and ate it sitting on the beach with her toes in the sand. While she did, she texted Leo to see if he was free to help her paint because she was woman enough to admit she was never going to finish it all today without help.

Because he was a good friend, he agreed to meet her back at the office. That, or he was grateful for the space to film. Either way, the afternoon passed pleasantly enough once she had someone to share the load. It also reminded her how much she genuinely liked Leo. He was like a Great Dane puppy tripping over his own paws all the time, but he was also sweet and funny and generally brightened any room he was in. Some part of Nora wanted to broach the topic of August and whether or not he'd miss her when he left. But it wasn't her place to pry, and she certainly didn't want to inadvertently cause trouble, so she left it alone, figuring he'd talk to her about it if he wanted to.

That night, she fell into bed so tired it hurt, but she was still thinking about the map and wondering where it led. She wondered, too, about the letter. Was it James Byrd that had set off Uncle Walter's feelings of unease, or was there something else afoot? And what had the wayward captain been looking for when he'd broken into her house? With the months ticking by on his measly one-year sentence, she felt compelled to figure it out long before he got out to try again.

Thankfully, Monday passed in a bit of a blur. She spent most of the day rounding up furniture for her new office space with Oliver's help. It might have been easier to order all new furniture and have it delivered, but it was infinitely more fun to hit the flea markets and antique shops to piece together something that was uniquely hers. Of course, the antique stores made her miss her friend Eve back in California, who happened to work in a shop much like the one Nora was standing in when nostalgia hit. Thinking about Eve made her miss all of her friends back in Lakeport, so she resolved herself to go back for a visit once things settled down.

In a case of impeccable timing, Gregory showed up just as Nora and Oliver finished putting the last piece of furniture in place.

"You planned that, didn't you?" Nora teased.

"Absolutely," he rejoined without missing a beat. He cast his gaze around the office, taking stock. "I like it. Very nautical."

"Thanks." She beamed. "It was getting harder and harder to run everything from the bookshop. I think this will help relieve some of the congestion."

"I have to admit, I'm curious to find out what you have planned for the *Amelia*."

Nora didn't have the heart to tell either of them that she didn't have the faintest clue what to do with the ship. Finding a captain had been a reflex. She'd just assumed Walter would have wanted her to get the boat back out there, but now she wasn't so certain.

"Oliver," she turned to the young man. "What was Byrd searching for the day I boarded the *Amelia*?"

He sat on the desk that would be Ivy's, thinking for a moment before responding. "He swore the wreckage of the

Golden Mermaid was in that area, that she'd been lost in a hurricane after attacking a merchant ship."

"But Walter thought the Spanish would have a claim to the treasure, so he didn't want to go after it, right?" Nora reached back into her memory to retrieve their conversation from that day.

"Right."

"Which means Walter either believed it was a Spanish galleon that went down, or the *Mermaid* had attacked the Spanish before she sank," Gregory surmised. "Either way, that would make it Spain's money."

Nora had struggled to make heads or tails of the laws surrounding salvaging wrecks—many seemed to contradict each other—but she did recall reading that merchant ships were treated differently than government vessels. There were different rules for each, and another set of rules depending on where the shipwreck was.

"I found a note from Walter," she began, deciding to only tell them part of the truth. "In it, he said he was concerned his boat was damaging the environment. Do you know why?"

Oliver shook his head and looked to Gregory, who didn't hesitate with his response.

"The blowers. To be honest, it was the one thing that gave me pause about working for you."

"Could you please elaborate?" she prompted.

"They work by forcing the propeller wash down to the seafloor, sweeping away sediment from an area, revealing what's beneath."

Nora considered his words. "So, it's like rock stacking?"

Oliver and Gregory met her with a quizzical stare, so she expounded.

"I used to hike on occasion—"

Gregory interrupted her with his chuckle.

"What?" Nora asked.

"I'm sorry, I can't picture that."

"Not by choice, but I did it and I did well." The scowl she fixed on him wasn't entirely serious. "But I remember being told that the pretty rock formations you'd sometimes see were actually bad for the environment. Some were supposed to be there, to guide hikers, but the random ones you'd see were bad because they destroyed the environment for native species."

"Something like that," he agreed. "And archeologists tend to get pretty touchy about the practice, too, because it destroys artifacts."

"Walter mentioned his findings belonging in a museum," Nora mused. She felt like she was beginning to see the full picture. She sat back, staring absently at the wall as she thought.

"So, whatcha thinkin' boss?" Oliver finally asked.

Nora sat up straight and sighed. "Get the *Amelia* out of dry dock and get her provisioned. Then start mapping the seafloor, starting in the area the former Captain Byrd had you looking."

"And then?" Gregory asked.

"For now, nothing. Check in with me when you get that whole area mapped out and we'll decide where to go from there. But don't use the mailboxes, even if you find something."

Both men nodded, and the conversation moved on to logistics of getting the boat ready and rounding her crew up. The question that now plagued Nora was this: How could she live up to the obligation she felt to provide this crew with gainful employment if she abandoned treasure hunting because it went against her conscience? She suspected Walter was grappling with the same question when he died.

At the moment, the only path to a solution was to keep moving forward until she had more information. To that end, the much-anticipated meeting with Arin Lancaster finally rolled around and Nora found herself dropping Margo at the shop with August so she could make her way to the lighthouse.

Situated at the north end of Anastasia Island in between Salt Run and the Matanzas River, the iconic lighthouse spiraled to the sky, black and white stripes chasing each other upward. The building had a red cap that most likely had a technical name, but Nora preferred to think of it as a cap. At its base sat a white house with a red roof.

"I'm here to see Arin Lancaster," Nora informed the woman at the front desk. "I have an appointment."

"Are you Nora?" the woman asked, looking up from her work.

"I am."

"I'm Arin. It's good to meet you."

Nora wasn't sure why it hadn't dawned on her Arin might be a woman. The name wasn't a typical spelling for either gender, so it could have been either.

"It's lovely to meet you Arin." Nora recovered from her initial confusion. "And thank you for taking the time to speak with me."

"Of course. Walter said you'd be by." She stood and walked over to retrieve something from a drawer on the back wall. "He asked me to give you this."

It was an envelope. Just a regular white envelope with nothing particularly special about it that Nora could see, save Walter's handwriting scrawled across the front. Nora took it and, remember her uncle's admonishment to be careful who she trusted, decided to wait until she was alone to read it.

"Thank you." Nora hesitated. It felt odd to just take the envelope and walk out. She took stock of the other woman—she was late thirties, early forties. Her long, golden blonde hair was pulled into a low ponytail. The kind Nora couldn't wear without looking like a founding father, but this woman pulled it off well enough. She wore a tank top and shorts; her skin was golden from time spent in the sun. "Did you know my uncle well?"

"To be honest, we met when I was protesting one of his recoveries. Most salvagers just lock horns with us. He listened to what we had to say and seemed to take it to heart. He asked to meet with me a couple more times, to learn what we do here. I might not agree with how he made his fortune, but I do believe he was a good man."

"He was," Nora agreed before asking. "What is it you do here, exactly?"

"We try to preserve Florida's history. Most people don't realize that our country wasn't founded on some New England coast—it started here. This city was founded more than fifty years before anybody stepped foot on Plymouth Rock. The battles fought here shaped this country."

"Yeah, I have to admit I had no idea the history of this place before I moved here," Nora admitted.

"Most people don't—and they don't realize how much history is sitting at the bottom of the ocean. Too many think of the sunken ships in terms of gold and jewels and not about the stories they tell."

His note to her was making more and more sense by the moment. She thanked Arin for her time and turned to go before pausing. "Just one more thing—do you know anything about a pirate ship called the *Golden Mermaid*?"

Arin's brow creased in thought. "No." She shook her head. "It sounds made up."

"I agree. Have you heard anything about wreckage here?" Nora walked over to a map of the coast that was hanging on the wall and pointed.

"There? Not that I can think of." Arin chewed her lip in thought. "Well, I mean, a while back some divers found a couple of cannons. They were most likely from a Spanish galleon, tossed overboard to lighten the load if they were sinking. We briefly sent a crew of archeologists out but never found more than the initial cannons. I never did agree with where they were searching, though."

"How so?"

"I don't think they properly accounted for changes in the coast—and that tides tend to move things south. Personally, I'd expect any wreckage to be more like…here." Arin walked over and pointed. "But that's just a guess. Please tell me you're not going to go desecrate another archeological find because of information I just gave you."

"No, I promise. I haven't quite figured out what I'm going to do with all of the things swirling about my head right now, but I will not be desecrating anything. Of that much, I am certain."

Nora thanked Arin for her time and left the lighthouse, waiting until she'd reached her car to open the envelope. It was coordinates. That's all. No note, no other instructions. Just coordinates. She tapped the coordinates into her phone, and it pulled up a map of an area known as Big Gum Swamp. Lovely.

Slightly frustrated, she headed to the nearest beach, where she kicked off her shoes and rolled up her pants, walking along the edge of the water and thinking. The only logical explanation was to apply the coordinates to the map he'd given her. But the bigger question in Nora's mind was if she wanted to go traipsing around a swamp by herself. Raymond might find her description of the Florida wilderness amusing, but Nora was still fairly certain there were things like alligators and bears and panthers out there—none of which she or Margo could take on.

Walter had warned her not to trust anyone, but in this regard, she felt she must overrule him. There was one person she trusted, even if she was irritated with him at the moment. So, she pulled out her phone and texted Rafael.

"Care to spend a day in the swamp with me?"

His reply was instant and only one word, but it made her smile. "Always."

CHAPTER SIX

THERE WAS A LOT MORE WAITING TO TREASURE HUNTING THAN ONE might expect. That's what Nora thought, anyway, as she made plans to set out with Rafael bright and early the next morning. Granted, it was only a day, and he was taking a personal day to make that happen, but still—she was itching to get started now.

The coordinates were two hours away and she had absolutely nothing to wear that was suitable for a swamp, so Nora decided to make use of her time. Besides, she'd been so busy this last week that she'd barely seen August.

"How do you feel about taking a long lunch and going shopping?" Nora asked upon entering the shop—after stooping to greet Margo, that is.

August glanced up from the books she was shelving. "I've never been much on mass consumerism, but the long lunch sound appealing."

Nora smiled at that entirely August answer. "The detective and I are going hiking tomorrow, and my wardrobe isn't exactly suitable." She couldn't help noting that August's wardrobe today consisted of a boho skirt and a t-shirt that said, "I used to be a people person then people ruined it for me." She wondered how the customers felt about that one. She was pretty sure they forgave August when she flashed that dimple of hers at them.

"So, hiking with the detective, huh? That sounds… exciting."

As badly as Nora wanted to fill August in on the whole affair, her uncle's warning rang in her ears. He hadn't known August. Surely, she was exempt from Walter's caution, but the more people she told, the more likely it was word would trickle back to whomever Walter had been concerned about. So, Nora smiled and dramatically rolled her eyes. "Not what I would have chosen for the day, but I'm still looking forward to it."

"Detective Medero doesn't strike me as the outdoorsy type," August observed.

"Me either." Nora wasn't sure how to explain his sudden interest away. Perhaps that's why she blurted out something she hadn't intended to share. "I was engaged to an outdoorsy man once, you know."

"I did not know." August straightened.

"He died, in a rock-climbing accident. I'd refused to go, so he took our dog with him, and I lost them both." Nora did her best to keep her voice light. She didn't think it would ever be an easy sentence to utter, but the blow it delivered had lost some of its sting over the years.

August blinked, trying to conceal the tears that sprang to her eyes. "That is the saddest thing I've ever heard."

"Surely not the saddest." Nora compulsively bent over to hug Margo once more, suddenly grateful for the sunshine the dog had brought into her world. "I've seen how you spend your days off—you and Charlotte have been volunteering with that ocean preservation group, haven't you? I imagine you hear sad things all the time."

"We have. And nice try, but you're not going to get me ranting about the state of our oceans right now. I think you and I had better go grab that lunch and see if we can find somewhere in town that sells hiking pants."

Nora glanced around the store. "Are we empty?"

"Yep. It's like a ghost town today, no pun intended. You know… because of Leo's show and all…"

"Yeah, I got it," Nora assured her.

"I was just going to work on putting all the romance novels back and maybe setting up a display on Irish fairytales."

"That's awfully specific."

"St. Patrick's Day is coming up," August said by way of explanation.

"Ah, gotcha. Maybe bring up anything we have that's Irish-y. I'm not sure we have enough to fill a whole display if we just do fairytales."

"The fae are more fun."

"Put them front and center then and use the rest for filler," Nora advised, amused at how August's mind worked. "Is Pru in the back?"

"She stopped by the studio on her way in. She should be here soon."

"All right, let's make a sign for the door, and I'll text Pru to ask her to open it back up when she gets here."

It didn't take long for them to get on the road. Their first stop was lunch—on a patio, so Margo could join. By the time they were done, Pru was back at the store, so they backtracked to drop the dog off.

"So, where exactly is he taking you?" August asked as they drove to the store.

Nora hesitated before deciding there was no harm in answering that much. "A place called Big Gum Swamp."

August was Googling before Nora had even finished her sentence. "Ooh, maybe he's taking you naked hiking."

"What?"

"Look." August held her phone out.

Nora glanced over. It was a picture of an older woman, naked as she stood behind a saw palmetto. "Oh my. That's certainly adventurous."

"I don't think you need to go shopping to go naked hiking."

"We're not going naked hiking."

"Are you sure? I mean, you didn't peg him for outdoorsy, either."

"I'm positive."

August didn't seem convinced, but she let the subject drop, instead choosing an article to read about the place. A few moments later, she began again. "Why on earth would he take you here? It sounds horrible. They say the ground is so boggy it's hard to walk. The place looks fairly deserted, except for deer hunters. Is it deer season? Maybe you should get something orange."

"Something orange?"

"So you don't get shot. Do you know nothing?"

"Not getting shot would be good. Orange it is."

"Not the whole outfit. Just, like, a vest or hat or something."

"Delightful." Nora's response was short because she was busy mentally cursing her uncle for sending her to the least welcoming spot in Florida in the middle of hunting season. She was beginning to suspect the map was something of his creation, made to conceal the real map.

August's teasing and Nora's hesitation over the entire venture aside, it was a pleasant shopping trip. It had been too long since the women had spent any real time together. By the end of the excursion, they had Nora successfully outfitted and they'd made plans for August and Charlotte to join Nora for dinner later in the week. Nora was missing the mini-adult, with those serious amber eyes and the riot of dark curls.

Once they got back to the shop, all three women worked together to get the displays moved. Nora enjoyed the time with them, and it helped the afternoon pass quickly. She spent her evening studying the swamp and trying to orient the map her uncle had left her with the map around the coordinates he'd given.

She went to bed early in hopes of being well-rested for her adventure, but sleep eluded, as it does whenever you want it most. Still, she was too excited to be resentful of her alarm when it went off the next morning.

Rafael showed up right on time, in hiking pants that looked every bit as new as hers. He was, however, driving a beat-up old blue Bronco that had seen its fair share of adventures.

"It's my brother's," he explained when he saw the curiosity on her face. "I didn't want to take my work car on this little adventure of ours."

"You'll have to thank your brother for me." She hoisted herself into the passenger seat.

"Will Margo be okay? I think that's the first time I've seen you leave her alone."

"August said she'd swing by to pick her up after she dropped Charlotte off at school," Nora explained.

Usually, there was an easiness to her friendship with Rafael, so she couldn't explain why she was such a bundle of nerves as they set out. Maybe it was because of their weird not-Valentine's dinner—or maybe it was because they were wading into unfamiliar territory for them both. Whatever the cause, the result was words tumbling out of Nora's mouth at an unprecedented rate she seemed to have no control over.

She talked about Leo's new show, about missing Charlotte, about whether or not August was going to settle in St. Augustine, and about Pru's new art studio. She rambled about her uncertainties over Mercury Enterprises, and whether she was adequately untangling the chaos her uncle had left or just making it worse. She told him all about Gregory Angelou and how he should be on the cover of a romance novel or something and how Oliver had done such a great job stepping up since Captain Byrd's arrest.

"So, you think your new captain is pretty perfect, huh?" Rafael asked quietly when she finally paused for breath.

"He is. He seems to be as good-hearted as he is handsome. I know it's terribly inappropriate of me, but I want to set him up with Ivy."

"Ivy?" It was hard not to notice how much his countenance brightened at that, which made Nora realize she'd been a complete dolt prattling on about Captain Angelou.

"Yes, Ivy." Nora weighed her next words. "You do know that when I said I wasn't ready to date, I wasn't just putting you off, right? I truly wasn't ready yet."

"Yet? Does that mean you are now?"

Nora opened her mouth to answer when she was distracted by a sign ahead. "Oh, look! We're here."

Rafael cut his eyes over to her but let it go, instead turning his attention back to navigating to their predetermined starting point. Nora's eyes soaked it all in. It looked much like she'd pictured it after studying everything on the internet, with tall, skinny pine trees soaring to the sky and sharp, pointy saw palmetto littering the ground below.

Though she'd been warned by her searches and by Raymond, Nora still felt ill-prepared for the massive mosquitos that swarmed the instant they were out of the car, intent on sucking the life out of both of their new victims. Nora felt like she'd bathed in bug spray and still her skin was welting up from the ones that got her right out of the gate. And she was reasonably sure nobody had bothered to warn her about the air that clung to them as they slogged along, thick enough to swim through. Nora didn't even want to think about what this trip would have felt like in the summer.

Nora had carefully laid a digital image of her map over the map of the coordinates last night, lining everything up and printing them a new, blended map of the two. And yet it did them little good as they stood in the middle of trees that looked nothing like the crisp, clean overhead view she held in her hand.

They bickered over how to translate it as they slogged through the miserable, spongey ground that made them work for every step. Sometimes, they'd be walking along on what they thought was solid ground, only for it to give way to a slough. At one point, she was certain they'd walked the same path three times. Any excitement they'd ever harbored had long since yielded to crankiness, but then Nora stopped short.

"Does that tree look like a snake to you?"

"It looks like a tree to me."

"What?" Nora didn't bother hiding her irritation. "It clearly looks like a snake."

"Why did you pose it as a question if you were so sure of the answer?"

"I suppose that cloud doesn't look like an elephant to you, either, does it?"

He followed her gaze, sighing. "It looks like a cumulus cloud."

"Next you're going to tell me you don't dream in color."

"Of course, I—" he stopped short, his brow creasing. "You know, now that I think about it, do I dream in color?"

"How do you not know?"

"Do you dream in color?"

"You poor man. I just don't even know what to make of everything I just found out about you."

"What did you just find out about me?"

"We don't have time for that now. Look." She pointed at the map. "It's a tree that looks like a snake. Like that one." She pointed at the tree and then at the map. "Which means we should find something if we walk fifty paces that way."

"If we walk fifty paces that way, we're finding an alligator." Rafael eyed the area skeptically.

She ignored him, counting out the steps until she found herself face to face with a large cypress tree with knees scattered around it, like anchors holding it in place, sticking their knobby little faces up out of the swamp to take a peek at the landscape around them.

"There." Nora pointed at one of the protrusions. "That one's different."

"One what?"

"The little cypress tree-knee-thingy. It's different."

He squinted, trying to see what she saw. "Different how?"

"The color. The texture. I don't think it's real. You should go check."

"I should go check?" At that, his eyebrows shot up.

"Yes. That feels like the gentlemanly thing to do."

"I'm pretty big on equal rights. You know there are alligators in there, right?"

"Oh, don't be such a baby. I don't think an alligator would want to take on a big, strapping man like you."

"Did you seriously just try to playground bully me and then immediately follow it with buttering me up?"

"Did it work?" She bit her lip and looked up at him hopefully.

"Why me? Isn't this your adventure?"

"I have the keener eye. I'm much more likely to spot an alligator if I'm lookout."

The look he gave her said he wasn't so sure about that, but he went to do her bidding, nonetheless, picking his way carefully over to the knobby protrusion in question.

"You're right—it's not real," he told her as he approached it, reaching down to cautiously feel for a way to pull it free. It popped loose into his grip, causing him to stumble back before he regained footing. He didn't pause to look his prize over, hightailing it out of the water before an alligator took exception to his presence.

"When you popped that thing loose, I half expected a gator to pop out of the water with it," Nora admitted, reaching for his hand to pull him the rest of the way out of the sludge. "If this had been a horror movie, you know it would have."

"Gee, thanks." His laugh was nervous. "I can't believe you talked me into doing that."

She joined his laughter even as his deepened with relief. They were still laughing when the first shot rang out.

"Ow! It nicked me." Nora twisted her arm just in time to see a patch of bright red appear. "And I'm wearing orange, too. I thought that was supposed to keep me from getting shot."

"That wasn't a hunting rifle." Rafael's face grew dark. "Come on—run!"

If walking through the spongey bog had been difficult, running was a nightmare. The ground alternately gave way beneath them and pulled at their feet, thwarting any real progress they might make. Her legs burned with the effort even more than her arm did from its brush with a bullet.

She didn't look back, she just ran, doing her best to keep up with Rafael so he wouldn't endanger himself by trying to wait for her. They made better time once they reached the firmer ground ringing the edge of the swamp. The pair zig-zagged in and out of the soaring pines, bullets whizzing past their head every so often and burrowing into trees when they missed their target.

By the time they reached the parking lot, both were drenched with sweat. Rafael fumbled with the keys briefly, swearing to himself as he struggled to get the door open. Once they were in, he tossed the fake tree he still clutched at Nora and cranked the engine, the old Bronco roaring to life. They were well on their way when they finally dared to look at each other.

Rafael looked back at the road and Nora closed her eyes, leaning her head back against the seat. "That… was horrible."

"What did we even find?" he asked.

"I swear to goodness if this is some kid's time capsule, I'm done."

Rafael chuckled. "If that's some kid's time capsule, he or she has my respect. That was some seriously scary water you had me wading through."

"It really was." Nora didn't even bother denying it.

"So?" he prompted. "What is it?"

"Oh, right." Nora loosened her grip on the oddly shaped canister and examined it for the first time. "We were right. It's not wood. It almost feels like rubber."

"Does it open?"

"I don't know. I'm trying."

"Here, let me see…"

Nora yanked it back when he reached for it. "You're driving, Mister Grabby Mc-Grabberson. Give me a minute."

"Well, there's got to be some sort of trigger or mechanism or something."

"One would think." Nora bit her lip in concentration as she studied the device before triumphantly twisting it apart. "Got it."

"What's in it?"

"It looks like rolled-up paper." Nora gingerly removed the pages from plastic wrapping and spread them out. "They're copies. They look like copies of old documents. Oh, wow. Look at this one—it's dated August 17, 1705."

"Wow. What do they say?" Rafael peeked over her way before returning his gaze to the road when she admonished him to be careful.

"I think… I think it's part of a ship's log."

"Why would your uncle stick an old ship's log in a fake cypress knee in the middle of an alligator-infested swamp?"

"He said he was worried about someone using his boat for ill. Maybe he didn't want them getting their hands on this?"

"Whoever it is, they must have assumed he'd point you in the right direction."

"So, what? They've just been watching me, waiting for me to find it?"

"Did you tell anyone where you were going today?"

"Only August, but she just thinks we're going hiking. I didn't tell her about the map."

"Why on earth does she think we're hiking in a swamp?"

Nora shrugged. "It's possible I let her think it was a date."

"She's going to think I come up with terrible dates." He frowned.

"Really? That's what we're worried about right now?"

"Well, you aren't. You're not the one planning dates in swamps."

"If it's any consolation, she was holding out hope that it was nude hiking," Nora said.

"I don't think I even want to know where that came from."

"Probably not. Some things can't be unseen."

Rafael looked at her, opening his mouth to speak, before closing it and turning back to the road.

"It doesn't look like we're being followed," Nora offered hopefully.

"Yet. We made it out of that swamp in impressive time."

"I was just trying to keep up with you."

"I wouldn't have left you," he promised.

"I know." Her voice was soft.

"I don't think you should go back home today."

"Don't tell me that. I want nothing more than my dog, a shower, and my bed."

"And to get your arm looked at," he added.

Nora twisted her arm, frowning at it. "It just grazed me. It stings, but I don't think it's worth a trip to the doctor."

"Will you at least let me clean it?"

"I would welcome the help."

"That's progress, I suppose."

"Are you okay? You didn't get shot or hurt or anything, did you?" Nora felt like a jerk for not asking sooner. The man had faced down an alligator for her, or had been willing to, anyway.

"I'm fine. So, are you insisting on going home right now?"

"I'd like to, yes, but if you think it's that dangerous, I won't. But—how long can I avoid my house? I mean, it won't be any safer tomorrow than it is today. Not until we figure out what this is all about and who we're up against, anyway."

Rafael's brow crinkled with concentration. He didn't respond right away. "You're right. Going home tomorrow won't be any better than going home tonight."

"So… does that mean I can go home, or am I moving?"

"You're adorable. Truly."

The tone of his voice said he did not think she was adorable at that moment, so she chose to ignore it and change the topic. "Do you read Spanish?"

"Did you really just ask me that?"

"Wouldn't it be rude of me to assume you did? Swearing in a particular language does not equate being literate in it."

"Fair enough," he conceded. "Yes, I do read Spanish."

"Good, then maybe after we clean up, you can help me translate what it is I'm reading here. Ninth grade Spanish is only getting me so far."

"It's in Spanish?"

"It is. Which raises a new question."

"What's that?"

"Why would a ship's log for a pirate ship off the coast of Florida be written in Spanish?"

"My guess is it wouldn't."

"Mine, too. So why would Captain Byrd tell everyone he was looking for a pirate ship if it was actually a Spanish galleon he was after?"

CHAPTER SEVEN

Nora hadn't been entirely honest with Rafael when she'd told him she'd defer to his wisdom when it came to whether or not they would return home. The truth was, she was tired and sore and shaken up, and she missed her house and her dog and her bed. If he had insisted that they stay in a random hotel in some random town, she might have cried.

As it was, she nearly wept with relief when they pulled into her driveway and Margo came running out to greet her. It was the longest she'd been away from the dog since coming to Florida and judging from the way Margo leaped and twirled around her feet, Nora had been missed.

"Sorry!" August called from the doorway. "Charlotte opened the door and Margo darted past."

"No harm done. I got her," Nora called back, looping a finger through Margo's collar just to be safe.

August let out a low whistle when she caught a good look at Nora and Rafael. "Wow. Looks like the swamp was even rougher than anticipated."

"It was," Nora agreed.

"But I did not get eaten by an alligator," Rafael offered.

"So, there's a bonus," Nora added.

"I considered it a good thing," he agreed. "Oh, and don't be surprised if a cruiser parks in your driveway soon. I texted Jonas and asked him to put a uniform on you for a day or two, just until we sort things out."

August looked from Nora to Rafael and back again. "There's something you're not telling me. What happened to your arm?"

Nora glanced down at Charlotte, who'd wrapped her arms around Nora's legs with a delighted squeal. "I'll tell you later."

"If you two are going to talk for a bit, then I think I'll go ahead and get cleaned up," Rafael said.

"There are towels under the sink in the master bathroom. You should have everything you need up there."

"Great, thanks." He lifted an overnight bag out of his backseat. "What? I came prepared."

"I didn't say a word." August held her hands up as if to show innocence, but her face was speaking volumes. "Hey, Charlotte, how about you let go of Nora's legs so she can come in the house?"

Nora took the little girl's hand in one hand, her other hand still firmly gripping the dog's collar, and the trio joined August inside.

"Have you guys eaten?" August asked.

"No, and I'm starving."

"Join me in the kitchen. I'll make you some dinner." August's tone left no room for debate, not that Nora was particularly inclined to argue it much.

Knowing her mother would put her to work if she stuck around, Charlotte went back to her television show. She might be four, but she knew how the world worked. Nora had barely settled herself on a stool when August put both hands on the island and looked Nora in the eye.

"Okay, girlie, spill it."

Nora considered her options before taking a deep breath and diving headfirst into the whole story, ending by fishing the hunk of fake tree out of her bag and setting it on the counter between them.

"This is what you found?" August reached out to pick it up, opening it with embarrassing ease. Nora told herself it's because she loosened it first. August carefully spread the contents of the canister out on the island, looking them over before speaking again. "I can't believe you didn't tell me."

"Walter told me not to trust anyone."

"I didn't even know Walter. And surely you can trust me."

"I think everyone says that in situations like these." Nora frowned. She didn't like hurting her first and dearest friend. "But I do trust you. I just know that every person I tell increases the chances of things getting to the one person I shouldn't tell. I was just trying to be careful. Fat lot of good it did me, though."

August gasped and threw a hand over her mouth.

Startled, Nora was instantly alert. "What?"

"Oh my gosh, Nora, maybe you can't trust me."

"Why on earth not?"

"I told Lucca where you were."

"What? Why?"

"He came by the shop, looking for you. I said you were on a hike with the detective, and he asked where. I thought he was just making conversation—I didn't know. I'm so sorry."

"Lucca?" Nora was devastated. She'd been so sure Lucca was one of the good guys. Well, not good per se, but that he'd meant her no harm.

"Now will you listen to reason about Lucca Buccio?" Rafael asked, entering the room looking refreshed from his shower. He also looked rather adorable with his wet, messy hair, but Nora was too irritated with him to acknowledge that.

"Of course, you had to hear that. You're going to be impossible to live with now, aren't you?"

"Live with?" August's eyebrows shot up.

"Be around," Nora quickly amended.

August patted Rafael's shoulder. "I'm rooting for you."

Nora stood up. "I can't with you people right now. I'm going to get a shower."

"And then I'm cleaning that arm of yours," Rafael called out to her retreating back. Nora didn't respond, but she did hear August say something about making dinner and Rafael offering to help.

The shower felt delightful, as they often do when you've gotten good and properly dirty. Not that Nora got good and properly dirty often. She allowed herself a few moments to savor the feel of the water on her skin, wicking away the stress even as it washed away the grime of the day. Her arm was beginning to throb, and the water caused it to sting anew. Some part of her wanted to curl up on her bed and cry, but she didn't see much point in caving in to the self-pity.

She forced herself to stop replaying the same moments over and over, refused to allow her thoughts to get on the hamster wheel in her brain where they'd just spin round and round, accomplishing nothing. No, she knew the most useful thing she could do at the moment was to focus on the shower. Her brain would be infinitely more useful after a break.

Nora couldn't vouch for her brain being any more useful as she padded down the steps in a pair of lounge pants and a t-shirt, but she did feel less like crying, so that was a win.

"That is the most human outfit I've ever seen you in," August commented, glancing up from the vegetables she was sautéing as Nora entered the kitchen.

"Are my clothes not usually human?"

"I am not touching that one," Rafael muttered, earning a scowl from Nora.

"You have a particular style, and you know it. I've never seen you in something that wasn't vintage."

"You have spent the night here before; you've seen me in pajamas."

"And even your robes look like something Greta Garbo would wear." August chuckled, amused at herself.

"You should let me take a look at that arm." Rafael deftly changed the subject. Nora complied, mostly because she knew he'd toss her over his shoulder and drag her to the hospital if she didn't. He led her to a chair at the kitchen table and instructed her to wait while he retrieved a first aid kit from his Bronco. She opened her mouth to tell him there was one in the bathroom, but he was already gone.

"That man can cook, too." August took the opportunity to get in yet another reason she felt Nora should date the detective. She'd been on a bit of a campaign as of late.

"How's Leo?"

It was Nora's standard deflection, but she felt bad for invoking it when she saw August blink rapidly a couple of times before answering. "He's great. Excited to get on the road. Promises he'll be back in the spring, but they're already trying to get him to go to the Pacific Northwest to track down some sea creature or another."

"I know the next few weeks will be hard, but I also know that man is crazy about you. I have to believe it's going to work out."

"You're sweet." August smiled. "But Leo and I are just friends. And Charlotte's getting to an age where she needs some stability. I was thinking about looking for an apartment here in St. Augustine. Do you think I could put you down as a reference?"

"Absolutely!" Nora bit back an offer to do more. August was a free spirit, but she was also fiercely independent. Nora didn't want to push her friend. It was just as well, anyway, because Rafael returned and set about cleaning her arm without preamble.

Nora pressed her lips together to keep from wincing as he worked.

"It's okay to say it hurts," he commented.

"If the roles were reversed, I'd tell you not to be such a baby about it."

"Most likely."

"I'm endeavoring to not be a hypocrite."

"A worthy endeavor."

"I thought so." Nora patted Margo, who had come to investigate her person's distress. "I think Margo is going to eat you for hurting me."

"Yes, she looks fearsome."

"Looks can be deceiving."

"They can."

"You're not going to start on the Lucca thing again, are you? Maybe the shop is bugged." Nora knew she was grasping at straws, but she wasn't prepared to admit defeat.

"Really? That seems more plausible to you than the mob boss being a bad guy?"

"Is there a way you can check?" Nora asked.

"If I check your shop for bugs tomorrow and it comes up clean, will you admit that Lucca is up to his eyeballs in this?"

"If you test the shop tomorrow and if it comes up clean, I would be willing to concede that it might be a possibility."

"That's the most I'm going to get out of you, isn't it?"

"It is." Nora smiled sweetly at him, forgetting for just a moment that her arm hurt.

"I like that," he commented.

"What?"

"Your smile. I haven't seen it much lately."

"I've been cross with you, haven't I?"

Rafael didn't answer her question. Instead, he smiled and placed a Band-Aid on her arm before declaring it all better.

Nora wanted to explain, to reassure him it wasn't anything he'd done, but rather her own fears made her hold him at arm's length. But she suspected he knew that and there were more pressing issues at hand, so she let it go. Instead, she simply grabbed his hand as he moved to pack away his things and said, "Thank you."

Things seemed almost normal as the four of them ate dinner that night. Charlotte chattered about her new school. Apparently, a boy named Joey had proposed but she turned him down because she was going to save the whales. They also learned that Miss Reid accidentally wore two different shoes to school, a fact she'd assuredly be thrilled to hear her students were sharing with their families.

"Mykal stopped by again today," August commented. "She brought the pastries that hadn't sold. Of course, Leo and Casimir were there, and they inhaled them."

"That was nice of her." Nora mentally chastised herself for not being more welcoming with their new neighbors.

"I think it had less to do with nice and more to do with making eyes at Leo. It feels like she's over any time he's around. Not that it matters to me. We're just friends. But still, how does she find time to run her own business?"

Nora let it go that nothing about August at the moment was saying "just friends." Instead, she cracked a grin and said, "Who knows? Maybe she's making eyes at Casimir? He assures me he's quite the catch."

August laughed, which is exactly what Nora had hoped for. Rafael gave her a confused look.

"If you met him, you'd understand," Nora offered by way of explanation.

"I have to admit, now I'm curious." Rafael leaned over to Charlotte. "What do you think of this Casimir guy?"

"He talks funny and pats me on the head. I don't like it."

"Well, there you have it. If Charlotte doesn't approve, I don't approve."

August smiled at him. "Wise man."

When the conversation circled back to the subject of the ship's log and what it meant, it was decided Nora would return to the lighthouse to see what Arin Lancaster thought about their find. Rafael offered to go with her, but Nora promptly reminded him he'd promised to sweep the shop for bugs.

"She's sweet, but she's bossy." August shrugged when Rafael opened his mouth to protest. "You know this about her."

"She's sitting right here," Nora protested, laughing.

"Aw, you know we love you." August stood and grinned, stretching her back. "But Charlotte and I had better scoot. All the good spots will be gone."

"You know you can stay here," Nora offered.

"Nah, you're too wild for us to hang with. You do remember you have a police guard right now, right?"

Nora shrugged. "I figured that made me the safest place in town."

"Uh-huh." August didn't bother to conceal her skepticism. "Have a good night, sweetie. Let me know if you need me to watch Margo while you go treasure hunting."

"I want to go treasure hunting," Charlotte declared sleepily.

"And someday you shall, but tomorrow you have to go to school so you can get super smart and save the whales," August reminded the little girl as she scooped her up.

Without asking, Rafael walked the pair to their van, opening doors so August wouldn't have to. He returned to find Nora curled up on the couch, already nearly asleep.

"Do you want me to stay here tonight?" he offered. "I happen to know your couch is quite comfortable."

Nora smiled at the memory. Only a few months before, he'd stayed on the couch because her home had been broken into. He was chivalrous like that. "I'm okay. You got me a protection detail, remember? Besides, you've got to be tired, too."

"I am," he admitted.

"Then go get some rest, silly."

"Okay." He didn't move from his spot.

"What?"

"You do look cute in casual."

"I look cute in casual?" She laughed, embarrassed.

"But my favorite was the overalls."

"When did you see me in overalls?"

"On the beach. Barefoot. Eating what looked an awful lot like a shrimp sticky rice bowl from my favorite food truck."

"You saw that?"

There was absolute mischief dancing in his eyes as he grinned. "Maybe."

"Why didn't you say hi? Stalker."

"You looked happy. If I'd said hi, you would have started worrying about being presentable."

Nora wanted to give a sassy retort, but she was tired, and he wasn't wrong.

He shrugged. "It's just good to see you let the armor down every now and then. Anyway, I'd better go. Early day tomorrow."

"Thank you, for everything." Nora wanted to give him a hug or at very least see him out, but her body wouldn't obey the command to get off the couch. In fact, the next thing she registered was Margo nudging her awake as sunlight trickled through her window. She'd slept on the couch, but somehow, she'd found a blanket and pillow. Nora suspected she had Rafael to thank for that, too.

She stumbled through making coffee and walking Margo, gingerly holding her arm as she tried to move it in circles to get rid of the throbbing. Then she took a cup of coffee to the rookie cop who'd been stuck guarding her for the graveyard shift before going to clean up.

Pru texted to say she'd be running too late to pick up breakfast after Nora had already parked, so Nora caved and stopped by her neighbor's shop to see what was fresh. Mykal seemed as surprised to see her as she was to be there. Between the brief conversation and the buttery croissant that melted in her mouth, Nora had to grudgingly admit that her new neighbors weren't the worst thing in the world. She still wished she could remember where she'd met Mykal before.

With her staff fed and her dog dropped off, Nora made a beeline for the lighthouse museum. She smiled at Arin, eager to share her find. The return greeting was not what she'd expected.

"Oh, no. I'm not talking to you again."

"What?" Nora blinked, surprised. "Why not?"

"You nearly got me chased out of here with torches and pitchforks last time. I'm new here—I nearly got fired for talking to a treasure hunter."

"But Walter sent me to talk to you. Surely you knew he was a treasure hunter."

"Walter and I shared a love for live music at Meehan's and sometimes we'd chat about archeology. He did not show up at the museum asking for help desecrating history."

"I'm not trying to desecrate history," Nora promised.

"Look, I want to help you. You seem nice and Walter was a good guy, but I can't get involved."

"Just take a peek at this and then I promise I'll leave you in peace."

"You found something?" Arin leaned forward.

"We did!" Nora glanced around to be sure they were alone before producing a folder from her bag and placing it on the counter in front of Arin.

Arin let out a low whistle as she ran her fingers gingerly over the pages. "They're gorgeous. I wonder how many hours of microfilm he had to sift through to find these."

"Do you know why Uncle Walter went to such great lengths to hide this?"

"I think this is from the *Francisca.*" She held up two of the pages. "Which means the wreck your captain was looking for was most definitely a Spanish warship."

"And subject to the Sunken Military Craft Act," Nora surmised.

"Exactly."

"So, he lied and said it was a pirate ship hoping to bypass years of litigation."

"There was a time a salvor could make decent money working with the state, but those days are gone."

"If half the treasures are claimed by foreign countries and the other half by the state or museums, why does anyone still hunt treasure?"

"Some would say it's in their blood–they can't help it. My boss says they read *Treasure Island* as a kid and never grew out of it."

Nora wondered if he had a point. There was an allure to treasure that wasn't necessarily rational. "Okay, well coming back to this treasure, you held up two pages—what are the others?"

"Well, this looks like a page from the port log in New York."

Nora looked again at the document. "How do you know New York?"

"There…" Arin tapped the page. Sure enough, she could make out the words "Port of New York" on it. She told herself the looping script made it harder to read.

"Here's another, from Caracas."

Nora struggled to process what it meant. "There has to be a reason Walter wanted to save this evidence."

"Don't look at me. I don't know why that man did half the things he did."

"Oh, but I have to look at you."

Arin's eyebrows shot up. "How so?"

"He sent me to you, specifically. So, I think you're the only one who can solve this. What's unique about you?"

"You mean, other than the fact that I'm a forty-five-year-old divorcee with grown kids who just took on an absurd amount of student loans to get a graduate degree in a male-dominated field? Or that the best job I could find after getting said degree was to work in a gift shop? There's the fact that I cut my pay in half on this little adventure, but I suspect I'm not the only woman to chuck it all in her forties, so maybe that doesn't make me especially unique."

"All of that sounds exactly like the sort of person my uncle would have taken under his wing."

The two women regarded each other for a moment before Arin relented. "Show me again."

Nora slid the papers back across the counter. Arin bent her head over them, studying them in silence for several excruciating moments before sighing and shaking her head. "I don't know. I'm sorry. And I'd like to help you, but you should go now."

Nora pulled a card out of her wallet and slid it to Arin. "Okay, but give me a call if you think of anything, okay?"

"Sure." The tone in Arin's voice didn't instill Nora with great confidence she'd be getting a call anytime soon. She left the museum with more questions than she'd had when she'd entered.

Why had Walter included port logs from two different cities, neither of which were close to St. Augustine? And how did pages from a ship log end up on dry land when the rest of the log—and the ship that contained it—were at the bottom of the ocean?

CHAPTER EIGHT

Disheartened, Nora headed back to the shop, wondering if there'd be one of those croissants left to console her. There wasn't, but Margo was so happy to see her it brightened her mood.

"Hey, boss," August greeted her in between helping customers. "Rafael came by earlier. He wanted me to let you know he didn't find anything."

Nora frowned, her mood plummeting again. "All right. Thanks."

Not that she wanted her store to be bugged—invasion of privacy isn't something one generally wishes for. But that did mean she had to concede Rafael might be right and her instincts about Lucca had been wrong.

She helped August in the front of the shop until the crowd died down, then made her way back to the office to see what Pru was up to. She was engrossed in something on the computer screen with noise-canceling headphones on, which usually signaled Pru was on sensory overload, so Nora didn't interrupt.

They'd gotten new advanced copies in since she'd last checked, so she snagged a rom-com and tossed it in her bag, hoping it might prove to be a sufficient diversion for the night. A bubble bath, a glass of wine, and a book was sounding like a fine way to spend the evening right about then.

Ivy swung by to get her key to the new office. She had another couple of weeks before she could start full-time, but she wanted to get started setting up her new space.

"Gregory asked if there was a time that he could swing by the office to fill out his paperwork," Nora told her.

Ivy's eyes lit up. Nora was certain helping someone fill out W-2s had never been more appealing to the woman.

"What's his story?"

"I only know bits and pieces," Nora answered truthfully. "He has a sister who owns two Goldendoodles that don't listen to him. He's left multiple jobs because he refuses to endanger his crew or the environment, so he has a conscience that he listens to. But other than that, I don't know."

"At least his tax forms will tell me if he's single or not."

"That's pretty brilliant. Morally gray, maybe, but brilliant."

"Morally gray? What?" Ivy rolled her eyes. "There is not a thing wrong with using the tools at my disposal to find out if the man is at least single. Tell me you didn't do an internet search on Detective Mc-Cutey-butt at some point."

"Touché," Nora conceded. "Well, after you're done sleuthing out Captain Angelou's marital status, can you file the paperwork on the Hummingbird stuff? I paid for Pru's rent. I thought she could be the first recipient.

"Aw, now, Nora, you can't be doing that to me. There's a procedure you have to follow to make it legit. You can't just go around writing checks like Mama Warbucks or something."

Nora was too amused at Ivy's reprimand to be stung by it. "Okay, well, take the rent out of my pay and never tell Pru it wasn't the grant. But I want to get everything set up so we can start using it."

Ivy pinned her with a look. "And I want to get your businesses on firm footing so we don't blow through your inheritance in the first year."

"See? This is why you're in charge of the money."

It was weird—it felt like there was so much going on and yet, in so many ways, it was an utterly ordinary day. Ivy left, customers came and went. Nora sent August home before they closed so she could get Charlotte picked up from preschool and the pair could do some apartment hunting.

Nora had her book and bubble bath on the brain when she went to flip the sign to closed, so it took a moment to register that Arin was practically skipping with excitement as she headed her way.

"I didn't expect to see you again," Nora said by way of greeting.

"August 1705." Arin beamed as the words spilled out of her mouth.

"Excuse me?"

"Care to join me for dinner? Because we need to talk about a Dutch pirate and a hurricane."

Nora still had no clue what the woman was talking about, but her curiosity was piqued. "Okay. I need to finish closing up the shop. Do you want to meet somewhere?"

"The Backyard Island Cafe. I'll go get us a table."

Nora promised to be along as soon as she could. She tried to hurry through closing, but the third time she miscounted a drawer, Pru shooed her away, promising to take care of the shop. It wasn't long before she and Margo were headed to the happy little patio with a beach party vibe.

She barely got her drink order in before Arin began talking. "I did some digging in my downtime today at work. I could not, for the life of me, figure out what Walter was trying to tell us with that random stack of papers. But then it hit me—Adrian Clavar. He was a Dutch pirate out of New York at the time. And in late August 1705, he came back from a raiding expedition in a Spanish ship."

"Okay." Nora wasn't sure where Arin was going with this, but she was intrigued.

"So, that made me wonder what was happening around that time in the other points on our map." Arin continued. "And records show there was a hurricane mid-August in 1705 that took out at least one Spanish ship. May I see the pages again?"

Nora hesitated. Every time she got them out, she envisioned them blowing away, getting a drink spilled on them, or some villain materializing to snatch them out of her hand. But she also knew they wouldn't give up their secrets tucked away in her bag, so she produced the folder she'd tucked them away in, sliding it across the table toward Arin.

The other woman leaned over, looking through each one more time. "There. A three-ship convoy left Caracas August 8, 1705."

"And at the end of August, a pirate captain sails back into New York with only one of the ships."

"Exactly." Arin's eyes shone with excitement.

"Which begs the question, where are the other two ships?"

"Their departure date would have put them in the path of that hurricane. I suspect at least one of them tried to make it to St. Augustine to ride out the storm."

"Why St. Augustine?" Nora asked.

"It would have been a gamble, but if they'd made it, it's a pretty decent hurricane hole for ships to weather storms. But if they get caught in the storm before they make it to the harbor, they'd have been in trouble."

"Judging from the canons pitched overboard, they did not make it," Nora surmised.

"So it would seem."

Nora bit her thumbnail in thought. "What about the other ship?"

"That's the billion-dollar question now, isn't it? Arin sat back to allow the server to place her drink on the table. Both women ordered and thanked the server, but neither cared much about drinks or food at the moment.

It occurred to Nora there was one more boat missing. "Wait, what about Clavar's boat? The one he sailed out in?"

"Excellent question. It's possible he got caught in the hurricane, too."

"How on earth would you find it then? That's a lot of seafloor to map."

"If you don't mind me taking pictures of the documents, I might be able to calculate a search area for you."

Nora looked down at the papers, befuddled. "How in heaven's name do you do that?"

"I can use the ship log to determine their rate of speed, factor in variability for the weather, and give you a basic box of where they could have been on what day. We know when the storm hit. Let me plot out their path and we'll see what that tells us."

"And you wondered why my uncle sent me to you." Nora was impressed. "All those times I asked my Algebra teacher when I'd ever use math in real life, and he never once replied 'treasure hunting.' I might have paid more attention if he had."

"Sailors used trigonometry to navigate along the coastline, you know," Arin told her.

Nora scooped up the pictures, replacing them in the folder and sliding the folder back in her bag. "I'd have been in real trouble, then. I got a D in Trig."

Arin laughed. It was a warm, light sound that made Nora smile. They spent the rest of dinner talking about a variety of things, like what brought each of them to Florida. Nora told her about leaving her life in San Francisco to come tie up loose ends when she'd inherited her uncle's estate.

"I wasn't sure I was going to stay," Nora remembered fondly. "But I fell in love with this place, these people. Now, it's home."

"I love that." Arin's smile was wistful. "I'm still figuring out where home is."

"Yeah? What brought you to sunny St. Augustine?"

"It was the only job I could find. As it turns out, it's hard to break into a new field when you're middle-aged, fresh out of grad school, and have zero experience."

"Switching fields is rough. I was so lucky this landed in my lap," Nora commiserated. "Where are you from originally?"

"New York. Upstate, not the city. I got married while I was finishing my bachelor's. Brian wanted me to stay home once the kids were born, so I never got a job with that shiny new degree. But then, he decided to go start family 2.0 about fifteen years later, so... I took a job teaching history at the high school. The pay was abysmal, but at least it let me keep similar hours as the kids. And then, when I was down to just one at home, I went back for my graduate degree. I figured it was time for me to do what I'd wanted to do twenty years ago."

"And what's that?"

"I want to be an archeologist. I want to explore and track down hidden pieces of human history and then share them with the world so we can learn from who we were."

"That is an amazing dream." Nora could see why Walter had taken such an interest in Arin. As strange as it sounds, he would have seen himself in her—he would have identified with that longing for adventure.

"I cannot believe I just told you all of that. What do they put in these drinks?" Arin eyed the fruity cocktail with suspicion. "It's not like me to spill my entire life story to a stranger."

"Nonsense." Nora smiled at her. "We all need to tell our story to someone at least once. I'm honored I got to hear it."

Still, Nora could tell that Arin was itching to get home so she could start her calculations, and she herself couldn't wait to talk to Rafael to tell him what they'd found. She was beginning to get paranoid, though—was it safe to text him? How difficult was it to clone a phone? The movies made it seem like any old person could intercept your calls and texts.

Rather than risk it, she arranged to meet him for coffee in the morning before work. Maybe Arin would have their coordinates by then. Probably not, but maybe. She had no clue how long that sort of thing took.

Nora and Margo headed home, where they spent the rest of the evening curled up on the couch, Margo chewing on her favorite blue ball and Nora researching the summer of 1705. She learned that it was a tricky time to be in Florida. To the west, they had French colonies, to the northeast, they had British colonies, and neither seemed to care for the Spanish, who happened to control Florida. Across the ocean, their parent countries were embroiled in a war over who would secede the Spanish throne.

Nora wondered what any of it had to do with a Dutch pirate out of New York. Perhaps nothing. Perhaps he'd merely been opportunistic. It was common knowledge that the Spaniards had been hauling gold out of South America for nearly two hundred years by that point, and pirates had been stealing it from them all along. Some sanctioned by their government in acts of covert war. Some just because they could.

When she finally went to bed that night, her head was filled with images of pirates and adventures on the high seas. By morning, she was bursting to talk to Rafael about what she'd learned.

She brewed a pot of coffee so she could take some out to the officer stuck watching her house a second night in a row.

"Thank you, ma'am." He beamed up at her from his seat, a dimple gracing his kind face.

"It's Nora—and thank you for taking such good care of me, Officer…" Nora paused, trying to read his badge.

"Davis. Rhett Davis, ma'am."

"It's nice to meet you, Officer Davis."

"You, too, ma'am."

"Nora."

"Yes ma'am."

"And this is Margo." Margo rested her nose on the car, looking up at the young man as if to say hello.

"Hello, Margo." His voice took the tone one gets when greeting a dog, and Nora liked him even more for that.

"Well, I'd better run. I'm going to be late. Have a good day." Nora turned to go, chuckling to herself when he called out behind her.

"You have a good day, too, ma'am."

She and Rafael met at a little coffee shop near the beach. When she arrived, he was leaning against his car with a coffee in either hand, waiting for her.

"The patio is closed, so I got our coffees."

"Oh, drat." Nora frowned. She'd been looking forward to sitting and visiting. "I mean, thank you for the coffee, but drat about the patio."

"I thought maybe we could go for a walk on the beach," he suggested.

She personally thought trying to juggle a dog's leash and her coffee sounded infinitely less pleasant, but she was game to give it a shot.

As they wandered, she told him about the conversation with Arin and that she hoped to have coordinates for them to start their search within the week.

"James Byrd must have known that your uncle found something. The log has to be what he broke in for," Rafael said.

"So, was he planning a mutiny or something? It was still my uncle's boat."

"Maybe he had a buyer lined up for the information. Someone with a boat of their own."

"You're still stuck on Lucca, aren't you?"

Rafael shrugged. "It would make sense."

"Does it, though? Is the mob big on looking for sunken treasure?"

"It's a huge source of funding for them."

"Treasure?"

"Artifacts."

"Really?" Nora was surprised. "Where do they sell them?

Auction houses? I would think museums verify what they display."

"Terror groups out of the Middle East use social media marketplaces to move their looted artifacts," he told her. "But the mob is a bit more refined. They forge documents of authenticity. Some go through auction houses, but some do go through museums."

"Interesting." Nora thought it over. "But that doesn't mean Lucca is behind this."

"It doesn't mean he's not, either." Rafael's words hung in the air.

CHAPTER NINE

Maybe Rafael's paranoia was getting to her because after they parted ways, she couldn't shake the feeling that she was being followed. She and Margo headed to the shop, looping around the block an extra time to test her theory. Nora knew she looked like a crazy person as she walked down the street, randomly stopping, turning, or dipping into alleyways to see if she could catch someone in the act.

She also knew that in all likelihood, if she was being followed, her pursuer would now be aware that he'd been busted, so her antics might have scared him off. Regardless, the feeling abated and she went to the bookshop, hoping it would provide a worthwhile distraction from all things treasure.

Pru was spending her day at the art studio, so Leo and crew were taking advantage of her absence to set about the noisy work of moving the recording equipment into the loft. Casimir sat on her counter, watching everyone else work with a look that reminded Nora of a bored king looking down on his subjects.

She knew that if she'd walked in to find Pru, Leo, or August sitting on her counter, she wouldn't have thought anything of it. But Casimir doing so irritated her. Perhaps it was petty, but she reminded him they were a business, and a customer might need to set books on the counter.

"Aw, babe. Don't be that way. You'd be so much prettier if you'd smile more."

She suspected he thought the grin he was giving her was infinitely more charming than it actually was. Nora didn't reply to his comment. Rather, she stopped what she was doing and fixed him with her gaze, arching an eyebrow and waiting for him to get off her counter.

After an awkward moment, he coughed uncomfortably and slid down from his perch. Nora turned, to go back to helping move books when a man walking past the store caught her attention. She was sure she'd seen him walk by just minutes before.

Telling herself she was imagining it, Nora hauled another stack of books up the stairs, handing them off to August to shelve before trotting back down the stairs for more. Two trips later, she saw the man walk by again, this time ducking into the shop next door.

Nora debated going next door to see how the guy would react. Before she could work up the nerve, he reemerged, locking eyes with Nora for a suspended moment before ducking his head and hurrying off.

It was driving her crazy—she knew she'd seen him somewhere before; she just couldn't place where. Even as she wracked her brain trying to remember, Mykal popped in the door with a cheerful smile.

"I come bearing gifts," she announced, holding up the boxes in her arms.

"Pru will be sad she missed this." Nora forced a smile. Maybe she was just unsettled by the mystery man, but the timing of the visit seemed suspect.

"So—" Mykal leaned in conspiratorially. "What's this I hear about you and Detective Medero going hiking?"

Nora shot August a look, who shrugged innocently.

"Oh, was I not supposed to know about that? Sorry. I overheard August mention it last time I was over."

"No, that's okay." Nora recovered. "We did go hiking. It was fun."

"Looks like you got scratched up." Mykal pointed to Nora's arm.

"Yes." Nora reflexively brought her hand up to cover the spot. "It's just a scratch. I'm a total klutz. Poor Raf probably regrets letting me tag along on his little adventure."

All three women laughed, but it felt stiff and awkward.

"What did you bring us?" Nora changed the conversation.

"Just some of those cucumber sandwiches that went over so well last time."

"Sounds wonderful. Are you sure I can't pay you for them?"

"Positive. They're a gift." Mykal's smile seemed so genuine, Nora wanted to soften toward the young woman. That is, until she spoke again. "Hey, is Leo around?"

"He is, but I think he's busy right now. He was rushing around, trying to get all the equipment moved before his date with August." Nora didn't feel even a little bit bad about lying right through her teeth.

"Oh. I didn't realize." Mykal laughed nervously. "I should get going anyway."

"Sure." Nora nodded, the tiniest bit of guilt blossoming in the pit of her stomach. "Thanks again for the sandwiches. I can't wait to try one."

August waited until they were alone before walking up alongside Nora. "I'm glad you're on my side."

"Oh, stop. I spoke before I thought. Now I feel like a jerk."

"I don't know. I appreciated it."

"It was instinct. You two are meant to be together, even if you're both too hardheaded to say it."

"Gee, thanks." August gave her a wry look. "You're not going to eat those sandwiches, are you? What if they're poison?"

"Rafael says the odds of having two murderous neighbors

are slim."

"He has a point."

They both stared at the sandwiches for a moment.

"Hey, Casimir!" Nora called. "Mykal brought you some sandwiches."

August erupted into a fit of giggles, holding her sides and gasping for air as she commented. "Like I said, I'm glad you're on my side."

Nora surprised herself by impulsively giving August a side-hug. "I will always be on your side."

"Aw, now you're gonna make me cry." August hugged her back.

The two women sighed, arms looped around each other's waists, resting their heads together for a moment before Nora straightened and pulled away.

"Okay, I have to go see a mob boss to ask him if he put a tail on me."

"You say that like it's running to the store for milk."

"Honestly, the way my body reacts to dairy, the milk is a more terrifying prospect."

"I did not need to know that."

Nora laughed, fishing her purse out from under the counter as she called for Margo.

"Are you okay to lock up?"

"I have to pick Charlotte up from preschool at four."

"Oh, right! I keep forgetting about preschool. Want me to swing back by here or pick up the kiddo?"

"I think I'll pick her up—just until you don't have mafia dudes trailing you, that is."

"Potentially trailing me, but fair point. I'll be back by three-thirty so you can get the munchkin."

The women said their goodbyes, but Nora's mind was already on the task ahead and what she could possibly say to Lucca. She supposed marching up and asking outright if he was following her would never do. At least she knew where he'd be.

The man was a fan of routine, and this time of day, he'd be having a slice of pie at his favorite diner.

By the time she parked her car, her nerves were in a proper state. She took a steadying breath before getting Margo out and walking into the diner with more confidence than she felt.

"Hey, you can't bring that dog in here," a kid called from behind the counter.

"Nora! Margo! My two favorite ladies." Lucca stood and held his arms wide, effectively silencing any protests over the dog being in the restaurant.

Nora plastered a smile on her face and greeted him with a hug and a kiss on the cheek. "Lucca, I thought I might find you here."

"Have a slice of pie with me?"

"No, thank you." She turned to the young man. "Could I get a coffee, black, please?"

The teenager scrambled to do as asked, and Nora felt bad for him. If he was this terrified of Lucca, this afternoon shift must be torture for him.

"So, to what do I owe the pleasure, my dear? I assume this is not a social call."

"Unfortunately, you assume correctly," Nora admitted, wondering if the man got tired of someone always wanting something from him. "I think I'm being followed, and I honestly didn't know who else to turn to."

"What about that handsome young detective you've been seeing?"

"Detective Medero and I are friends." At this point, the protest was reflexive more than heartfelt.

He smiled and patted her hand. "I think everyone but you knows that isn't true."

"At any rate, he put police protection on my house, but I think someone's following me throughout the day and I don't think it's fair to ask for more police resources. I mean, they aren't my personal bodyguards."

"Would you like a bodyguard? That can be arranged," he offered.

Nora paled at the thought of Rafael's reaction if she had a low-level mafia thug acting as a bodyguard the next time that he saw her. "I don't think that's necessary; I don't want to put you out. I just, I didn't know who else to turn to. What do I do?"

Nora didn't hear his reply because a man rose from the corner table and walked toward them. She froze like a deer in headlights; it was him. The man she'd locked eyes with at the store, now gave her a cool glare as he leaned down and whispered something in Lucca's ear.

With sickening clarity, Nora saw everything in a new light. She rose, backing away even as she said, "You know what? I'm sorry I bothered you with this. Thanks for the coffee."

She didn't have to encourage Margo to leave; the dog was terrified of Lucca and eager to be out of there. Nora had always chalked Margo's fear up to memories of her racing days, but maybe she shouldn't have written off the dog's reaction so hastily.

Nora headed straight home from the diner. Even if there wasn't a patrol car camped out front because nobody expected her to be there yet, it still felt like the safest place to be. When she got to her driveway, she paused to text August, asking her to just close up early because she wouldn't be back. She was shaking so badly she could barely type; she was in no shape for working.

Once inside, Nora paced back and forth for a while, trying to make sense of how badly she'd misjudged Lucca. Clearly, stereotypes were a thing for a reason. As she paced, she took inventory of potential weapons in each room. She wasn't a gun kind of girl, but she had no qualms hitting someone over the head with a hefty candlestick or something. If the game of Clue was to be believed, candlesticks could be quite fearsome weapons.

Her pacing was beginning to make Margo nervous, so she put on a kettle for tea, deciding that maybe a cup of something soothing and the book she'd brought home might do the trick.

Sure, she should immediately call Rafael and tell him what was going on but sticking her head in the sand sounded like a good option, too.

The doorbell rang, causing Nora to nearly jump out of her skin. She peeked through the hole in the door, her breath catching when she realized it was Lucca. Perhaps coming home alone hadn't been her best choice. She briefly debated darting out the back door, but if he intended her harm, he'd have that door covered. There wasn't much of an option other than opening the door and trying to not look terrified.

"Nora, dear," he greeted her warmly. "Lorenzo told me you spotted him outside your shop today. I can only imagine what you must be thinking."

"Can you?"

"May I come in? I believe we should talk."

"If you truly know what's going through my brain right now, how can you expect me to let you in?"

He opened his arms wide. "I am unarmed and alone."

A sharp whistle split the air, causing Nora to jump again. She was beginning to get irritated with herself for the habit.

"You can hit me over the head with your hot tea kettle if I threaten you in any way," he offered.

Nora narrowed her eyes but stood aside to let him pass.

"Would you like some tea?" she asked, heading to the kitchen and snagging a spearmint tea bag for herself.

"What do you have?"

She slid a basket full of teas his way.

He rummaged through, producing a raspberry chai and handing it over to her. "I think you should know, Lorenzo was not following you."

"No?" Nora arched an eyebrow, not convinced.

"He was there to speak to Mykal."

"Why does that do nothing to reassure me?"

"I believe Mykal is my daughter."

Nora blinked, trying to process the bomb he'd just dropped. "Does... does Mykal know?"

"Lorenzo was there trying to ascertain as much."

Nora had a million questions, but it didn't seem right to press him on the subject. He'd tell her what he wanted her to know. Now that he'd said it, she could see it—and it explained why Mykal felt so familiar. She looked like her father.

"Her mother was quite special to me, but she did not approve of my occupation. One day, she just up and moved. My sources tell me she settled in Louisville, had a daughter—Mykal—and lived a quiet life. I checked on her from time to time but respected her wishes and kept my distance. I always wondered if the girl was mine. But when she just up and moved to St. Augustine, of all places, my suspicion grew."

Nora pulled a stool around to her side of the island and sank onto it. "Does Lorenzo think she knows?"

"He's not sure. She's played her reasons for coming pretty close to the vest."

"I can try to find out for you," Nora blurted. "If you'd like, that is."

"Ten minutes ago, you were worried I might try to kill you."

"Rafael says befriending you is like having a wild animal for a pet; you can never be completely certain it won't someday turn on you."

A wounded look crossed his face, but he eventually murmured, "I suppose there is some truth in that, however much I would like it not to be so. I can't blame your detective for wanting to protect you, even if it's from me."

"Even if it wasn't Lorenzo, someone is following me. They showed up at Big Gum Swamp, they were following me yesterday. Who knows when and where else they've been?"

"Is that what happened to your arm?"

"A bullet grazed me that day in the swamp."

"My dear, I believe you've encountered the Garduña, much like your uncle and I did years ago."

"The what?"

"They are an ancient secret society in Spain. They've been doing their government's dirty work for more than four hundred years—including the Spanish Inquisition."

Once upon a time, Nora had thought having the mafia on her tail was the scariest possible outcome. Now she longed for the naïveté of five minutes ago.

"We were an improbable pairing, your uncle and I."

"I've often wondered what brought the two of you together."

"It was the late 80s. He was a gay man from San Francisco, I was a wise guy fresh from New York. We should not have been friends. But we got to talking about boats one day, and we just clicked, you know? He had big dreams. He said the coast was littered with treasure, and he aimed to find some of it."

"He left me a note, told me the two of you set out."

"Nah, he did the sailing. I was just the money man. I raised the capital to get him on the water. In return, he promised me a percentage of his findings, paid annually. But the real payment was getting to live his adventures vicariously through him. And they were grand adventures, indeed."

"He wanted me to go on an adventure," Nora found herself saying. "He gave me a map, that led me to another map, of sorts. It's why I'm being followed."

"Then they are back." Lucca's face was grave.

"You said that you and Walter tangled with them before?"

"When Walter got his start, it was before a treasure's ownership was settled through court battles. It didn't occur to anyone that the Spanish treasure sitting at the bottom of our ocean might still belong to them. Well, to anyone except to Spain. They still felt they had a right to it. So, they sent the Garduña to claim it."

"What happened?"

He shrugged as if it were of no consequence. "We protected our investments. The Garduña were not expecting the treasure to be guarded by the family. When they realized it was, they acquiesced."

"But, if treasure claims are decided by court battles now, why would Spain send the Garduña after me now?"

"Court battles are lengthy—and expensive. It's possible they're tired of discussing it."

"Wonderful." Nora took a sip of her tea, which had cooled while sitting ignored. Her doorbell rang, and she excused herself to go answer it. She could tell even through the tiny peephole that the man on the other side of it was not happy.

"Rafael," she greeted as the door swung open.

"Are you okay?"

"Yes, I—"

"I swear, one of these days, I'm going to kill you myself."

"I believe that kind of statement might be considered a red flag in a relationship," she informed him calmly.

"Nora, when I got the call that Lucca Buccio's car was parked in your driveway, it took ten years off my life. I don't even want to discuss the laws I broke getting over here."

Lucca, having heard Rafael's voice, joined them in the living room and interjected into the conversation. "That is my fault, Detective. I came over to explain a misunderstanding between us."

"Care to explain it to me?" Rafael asked.

"I prefer to keep private matters private, but I promise you, I meant Nora no harm." He placed a hand on Nora's shoulder and looked down at her. "I trust you'll keep what I've told you to yourself."

She met his gaze. "And I trust you won't tell anyone about the map."

Once Rafael and Nora were alone, he blurted, "You told him about the map?"

"Come in; we should talk." She wondered just how to tell him Lucca's suspicion without sounding crazy. It's not every day one finds out they're being stalked by an ancient secret society responsible for the horrors of the Spanish inquisition, after all.

CHAPTER TEN

IT HAD TAKEN A WHILE TO CALM RAFAEL DOWN AFTER LUCCA LEFT the night before. Nora wasn't sure he ever did buy into her reasoning, but she stood by it. If Lucca was the villain in this particular tale, then he already knew about the map, and telling him garnered trust that might lull him into making a mistake. If he wasn't, then they'd just learned important information they wouldn't have otherwise known.

Everything Lucca told her tracked with what she'd learned from Walter. And, yes, she did want to believe he was telling the truth. But, whatever her feelings, the next logical step was to verify his story about Mykal. That seemed easier than trying to prove the existence of a mythological society that no two historians could agree on.

And while Rafael's anger had abated, his insistence that he follow Nora pretty much everywhere until this blew over had not. She wondered if the city was going to start billing her for their officers' time.

To that end, she put on a pot of coffee for Officer Davis, who'd drawn the short straw yet again—he'd spent his night sitting in a patrol car in her driveway. When Rafael arrived, she greeted him with a cheerful hello, determined not to let all the bickering they'd been doing affect their friendship.

"I'll just be a minute," she told him after ushering him in. "The coffee is just about finished brewing."

"Coffee? I thought we were swinging by Mykal's place."

"We are. This is for Officer Davis."

"Do you take him coffee every morning?"

"Mm-hmm." She fished a thermos out of the cupboard.

"At the end of his shift?"

Realization dawned on her. Without saying another word, she marched out the front door and down to the driver's side of the patrol car. Rafael followed right on her heels, undoubtedly curious. Officer Davis rolled his window down as she approached, greeting her with his usual smile.

"You're going home to go to bed after you leave here, aren't you?" she asked him.

"Yes ma'am," he admitted sheepishly.

"I am such a dope. You should have said something."

"No, I like the coffee you bring me. I save it for when I wake up," he assured her.

"I should bring you something like sleepy tea in the morning." Nora couldn't believe she hadn't thought of it sooner.

"Sleepy tea?" Rafael asked, his amusement growing with the conversation.

"Valerian root." Nora made a face at him.

"Ah. Silly me."

"You don't have to bring me anything, ma'am."

"Okay, first of all, call me Nora. Second, it's the least I can do. You keep me safe."

"It is his job," Rafael reminded her gently.

"And he does it well."

"Thank you, ma'am."

She pursed her lips and furrowed her brow. "I'm not going to get you to stop calling me ma'am, am I?"

"No ma'am."

Nora took a deep breath and let it out in a sigh. "Okay, well, I'm going to make you some tea for when you get home from now on, and I'll start bringing the coffee at the beginning of your shift."

"Thank you, ma'am."

She wished him a good day, intentionally ignoring Rafael's chuckle as he followed her back into the house. She gathered her purse and snapped Margo's leash into place, holding a hand up to Rafael when he opened his mouth to speak.

"Not one word."

"Yes, ma'am." Highly amused with himself, he giggled like a school girl at that. She told him as much as she breezed by, leaving him to lock up the house.

At his insistence, she agreed to ride in his car. He didn't trust Nora not to skip out on him if she had her own vehicle. So, even though she muttered about him patronizing her the entire time, she dutifully moved Margo's seat over to Rafael's Chevy Tahoe.

Margo, however, had other ideas. When Nora told her to load up, the dog sat down, looking quite elegant as she stared at them and refused to budge.

"What do we do?" Rafael asked.

"In my experience, life is easier if you don't disrupt her routine." Nora booped Margo on the nose and smiled. She was completely smitten with the animal, even if she was as stubborn as a mule. "If you want her in the car, you're going to have to hoist her in."

"Will she bite me?"

"Probably not."

"Prob—never mind." Rafael knelt beside Margo, talking to her as one would a child before lifting her into her seat and fastening the belt.

"What a good girl," Nora praised.

"The dog or me?"

"Both."

"Maybe if we get her stairs, she could climb into the seat," Rafael mused.

"That would be a no-go. She doesn't like stairs. Other than the ones that lead to her room."

"Of course she doesn't."

Nora clambered into her seat with as much grace as she could muster, looking every bit the queen by the time she fastened her seatbelt. "I like a woman who knows her mind."

"Of course you do." He repeated with a sigh, putting the car in reverse and glancing over his shoulder as he backed down the driveway.

As they made their way the short distance over to St. George Street, Nora couldn't help wondering, "Does it seem weird, Lucca having a daughter?"

"Allegedly."

Nora ignored the comment. "Do you think that's why she chose a place next door to me?"

"Or she chose it because it was open. You're really struggling to trust her, aren't you?"

"I think I would struggle to trust anyone taking over that shop, and through no fault of their own. It's completely irrational, I know," she admitted.

"You should cut yourself some slack. Things have been a bit of a whirlwind since you arrived."

"Thanks for saying that." Nora meant it, too. His opinion mattered. She spent the rest of the drive wondering what she should say. To her knowledge, there was no official etiquette for asking someone if the local mob boss was their long-lost father.

As it turned out, she didn't need to worry about what she'd say. Because Rafael Medero had apparently decided the correct approach was to just come right out and ask.

"I'm sorry, what?" Mykal blinked at him, glancing over to Nora as if she might give some clue as to what he was talking about.

"I asked if it was possible that Lucca Buccio is your father," he repeated. "Your mother is Terra Ellis, correct?"

"Mom?!?" Mykal called out, rather than offer up an answer. "Can you come out here, please?"

A woman who looked only slightly older than Mykal appeared from the back, still drying her hands. Nora had thought Mykal looked like her father, but now she could see much of her mother in the young woman, too.

"Can I help you?" Terra asked.

"Our neighbor and this cop want to know who my father is," Mykal told her.

Nora gave Rafael a look that she hoped was appropriately scathing before turning back to Mykal. "I am so sorry. I was just going to try to get a feel for why you came to Florida."

"And I took the more direct approach because I'm tired of people taking literal shots at you," Rafael defended.

"It was only the once." Nora frowned.

Mykal held up a hand. "You were shot?"

"Grazed. It was nothing."

"What does my father have to do with you being shot?"

"Maybe nothing." Nora shrugged.

"Maybe everything." Terra stepped up, having watched the conversation up until now like it was a tennis match. "Mykal, they're asking because your father is Lucca Buccio."

"Am I supposed to know that name?"

"He's a mob boss. Certainly the type of man who'd take a shot at someone—or tell one of his gorillas to, rather."

"Why would he shoot at Nora?" Mykal asked.

"Because I may have something he wants," Nora answered. "But last night, he told me it wasn't him. That he's been hanging around, that his men have been hanging around, because of you."

"So, he knows I'm his daughter?"

Terra paled. "I didn't think so. I left before you were born. Nobody knew I was even pregnant."

"He suspects, but he's kept his distance trying to respect your mother's wishes," Nora said.

"I always wondered why we didn't talk about my father. Who he was, where he was." Mykal looked like she wanted to sink to the ground under the weight of the news.

Rafael rushed forward with a chair, guiding her to it. "I'm sorry; I didn't mean to be an inconsiderate lug."

"No, it's okay. You were worried about someone you love. I get it," Mykal reassured him. Nora's breath caught at the mention of love. Rafael hadn't corrected her, but surely it was because it would have made the moment weird. Well, weirder.

"Mykal, I am so sorry we did this to you." Nora was awash with guilt. Mykal was being so kind and understanding about everything. Pru had been right about her all along, but Nora and August had been too stubborn to see it, though each for their own reasons.

Mykal didn't respond, instead looking to her mother. "Is this why we moved here? Opened this place?"

"I suppose I missed him, in some way. I wanted you to know him, someday—though this is not how I envisioned this conversation happening." Terra shook her head as if to clear it. "But mostly, I just missed this place. I mean, where else can you live and expect daily encounters with pirates just out and about on the street?"

Nora did appreciate the pirate presence in St. Augustine. Especially since these pirates were much more likely to raise money for charity than to pillage and plunder.

"We should go," Rafael suggested. "You two have a lot to talk about."

"Wait," Mykal called out. "I still don't understand. How does all of this help you get to the bottom of who's trying to hurt Nora?"

"It corroborates his story, which means there's a chance his theory about who is after her might be true, too," Rafael said.

"And maybe I'm the one who's right about him?" Nora gave

Rafael a look, silently beseeching him to at least consider the notion.

"How so?" Mykal asked.

Nora turned to Mykal. "I think he's a good man. I mean, as good as a man can be given his occupation. He was friends with my uncle, and he's been good to me. He's loyal. I don't think he'd hurt me."

"I agree," Terra interjected. "He's loyal to a fault. If he's decided you are family, he'd die for you. I didn't take Mykal away from here to get away from him. I took her away from his world."

"Thank you." Nora looked directly at Terra. "And it was lovely to meet you. I am sorry about all of this."

Terra nodded. Neither woman was shooting her death glares, but she still had the sense they might need to pick a different breakfast spot for the time being.

As soon as they were out the door, she turned to Rafael. "You get to tell Prudence that we've been banned from her favorite breakfast spot."

"Oh, look at the time—" He dodged the smack he sensed coming his way, making tracks down the street back to his car.

Nora bit her lip to keep from smiling and pushed the door open.

"Why was Rafael running away?" Pru asked curiously in lieu of hello. She, August, and Leo stood lined up along the storefront's large window, watching Rafael move away from the shop with impressive speed.

"Because he didn't want to be the one to tell you he just got us banned from Mykal's."

"What?" Pru shrieked.

Nora took a deep breath and dove into the explanation, realizing belatedly that she had yet to tell Pru or Leo about the map. Leo was so completely nonplussed by the news that Nora could only assume August had already filled him in.

"And you couldn't get us one last breakfast before you dropped a bomb on the poor girl's life?" Leo asked.

"I didn't drop the bomb," Nora retorted.

"And Rafael only did because he la-oves her." August sang the word "loves" like they were in third grade.

Nora cut an irritated glance at August but let it go. "I will order breakfast from anywhere in the city that you like. Just pick a place and get me your order. We'll have it delivered."

Deciding it was best to be the one to break the news to Lucca, Nora pulled out her phone and texted him. "Mykal knows... now." After thinking about it for a moment, she added the little emoji of a shrugging woman and hit send before she could lose her nerve.

She half expected him to immediately call back, but she suspected he didn't use his phone often. He was more of an in-person conversation kind of guy. The thought of having this particular conversation with him in person sent a shiver down her spine, though. Maybe she should just move. To Antarctica.

The bell above the door tinkled merrily, announcing someone's arrival. The four of them turned to see who it was, August murmuring her appreciation for the visitor even as Nora noted he was an especially well-dressed bookshop customer.

The man wore a pale gray Armani suit. His thick, dark hair was brushed neatly but looked like it wanted to rebel and escape its confines. He had dark eyes and long black lashes that any woman would kill for.

"May I help you?" Nora asked.

When the man responded, it was with such a strong accent that Nora could barely understand him. "I am looking for Nora Jones."

Lucca's warning of a Spanish secret society flashed through Nora's mind even as she stepped forward. "That would be me. What can I do for you?"

"May we talk? In private?"

"I don't think so." August stepped forward, and for a second, Nora thought her friend might try to remove him forcibly.

"It's okay, August." Nora held up a staying hand. "Follow me, Mr.—I'm sorry, I don't think I caught your name."

"Pérez. Sebastián Pérez." He produced a card and handed it to her. It was in Spanish, but she could read well enough to gather he was an attorney.

She handed the card to August and smiled reassuringly. If she wound up dead, at least they'd have something with the man's fingerprints on it.

Nora took her seat in the office, gesturing at the open chair. Once they were situated, he began without preamble.

"I represent the Spanish government in certain interests here in Florida."

"Such as?"

"Recovery of lost assets."

"I see." Nora briefly wondered who represented the people of Peru, where the treasures often originated.

"It's come to our attention that you are in possession of a map, a map leading to something that belongs to us."

"Come to your attention how?" she asked.

"How is not of consequence." He waved her question off as if it was a gnat buzzing around his face.

"I don't know—" Nora rested her elbows on the arms of her chair, resting her chin lightly on the steeple of her fingers. "I feel like it's of great consequence if I have secret Spanish henchman after me."

"Henchman?" He raised his eyebrows in question.

"The Garduña," she supplied.

"Ah. I see you have spoken with Señor Buccio." He pressed his lips together for a moment. "Let me tell you a story of three brothers, three Garduña. After being cast out of Spain for their bloody misdeeds, they were pirates for a time, right here in your Americas, before being shipwrecked on the island of Favignana, near Sicily. One brother, Mastrosso, made his way to Calabria and founded the 'Ndrangheta, one of the most powerful crime syndicates in the world. The second brother, Carcanosso, made his way to Naples, where he founded the Camorra, another large crime syndicate. The third brother, Osso, stayed in Sicily, where he founded the Cosa Nostra."

"The mafia," Nora breathed the words.

Sebastián leveled his gaze on Nora. "I do not believe your friend Lucca Buccio is as innocent in this as he claims to be."

CHAPTER ELEVEN

Sebastián Pérez's words chased each other around and around Nora's brain long after he'd gone. Every time she felt like her trust in Lucca had been justified, something came right behind it to shake her confidence again.

The two men were each pointing the finger at the other, and both made valid points. Nora knew that Rafael would use the Spanish attorney's visit to further his argument that Lucca wasn't to be trusted. She wasn't ready to give up on him just yet, though. She wasn't ready to trust him yet, either.

Before leaving, Sebastián offered her twenty-five percent as a recovery fee should the ship prove to be Spanish, which they both knew it was. The thing he didn't seem to know is that there was more than one ship. Nora suspected that if he found out, he'd be angling to take the finds from all three ships, and proving that one of them belonged to a Dutch pirate could tie the whole thing up in court for years.

It all depended on what search area Arin came back with, but there was a good chance the remaining two ships could be in international waters, making them subject to the Law of Finds, which meant they'd be fair game. What she needed was a way to keep everyone distracted while she figured out what she was dealing with.

Out of nowhere, Nora had an idea. She did some frantic Googling before she decided it was brilliant. Closing her laptop with more force than intended, she went in search of Leo, finding him in the loft, setting up the sound equipment.

"Leo, my friend—" She sidled up to him and rested her head on his shoulder, looking up at him beseechingly.

"Uh-oh."

"I'm wounded." Nora briefly pretended to pout before pulling back and affixing him with a smile. "I have an opportunity for you."

"Is that so?"

"You don't leave for a few more weeks, right?"

"Yeah…" he answered cautiously.

"How would you like to use the *Amelia* to spend some of that time searching for a sea monster?"

"To be honest, I was kind of hoping to have some downtime to hang out with August and Charlotte."

Nora held her hands to her heart. "I adore that answer. But I need a cover story. What if you ride out on the *Amelia*, shoot enough footage to pretend you're out there for a few weeks over the course of a few days, and then I sneak you back to shore?"

"What exactly are you cooking up here?"

"It can take years to find a treasure, even if you know where to look. So, it's possible I'm just being crazy here. But I need to get everyone off my back—or rather, off the *Amelia's* back—so she can find something for me."

"I think you'd better back up a few steps. I'm lost." He hopped up on a table and waited for her to explain.

"Everyone knows there's a Spanish ship that sank in U.S. waters off the Florida coast. I want to take the *Magnolia Jane* out to look for that."

"Isn't that Lucca's boat?"

"It is. He doesn't know it yet, but he's going to loan it to me."

"Isn't he one of your suspects?"

"He is, but a tiger by the tail and all that. If I have him with me and promise Spain seventy-five percent of what I find, it should remove the need for anyone to resort to nefarious deeds."

"Um... okay. Go on."

"What they don't realize is that Walter didn't give me a map to that ship."

"He didn't?"

"No, he gave me a map to two other ships, further out at sea. Those ships are worth tens of millions of dollars—and I don't have to split the find with Spain if I'm right about where they are."

"I like the sound of that." He motioned with his hand, encouraging her to go on.

"Whoever is following me—whether it's Spain, Lucca, or the boogeyman—"

"The boogeyman?"

"Don't interrupt."

"Right, sorry."

"Whoever it is," she continued, "if they catch wind of these ships, I'll have competition for them. Fierce competition. The kind that shoots at me. But if everyone thinks you've leased the *Amelia* to go hunt a sea monster..."

"Then you're free to search for treasure without dodging bullets."

"Exactly!" She beamed at him. "Even better, St. Augustine has a sea monster."

"Naturally." He chuckled. "This town is a treasure trove for the paranormal."

"You could just stay here for your show," Nora suggested. "I know August would like that."

Leo blushed and ran a hand through his hair. "I don't know about that. August is... August is amazing, but I don't think she sees me that way."

Nora bit her tongue. Her brain screamed not to get involved, even as she desperately wanted to get involved. Finally, she blurted, "She's as crazy about you as you are her. She's just scared. Don't you dare let her slip through your fingers and don't you dare tell her I said something."

With that, she scurried downstairs before he could gather his wits to respond. She belatedly realized she'd never gotten an answer from him about her plan, but she had other pieces to put in place anyway. His response could wait.

She had bigger problems at the moment. After briefly debating what she'd tackle first, she gathered her things and had made it so far as the door when she remembered Rafael had driven her to work.

"You just remembered you don't have a car, didn't you?" August asked, a grin playing on her lips.

"I did." Nora bit her thumbnail thinking.

"Would you like a ride?"

"Very much."

"I'll go ask Pru to cover the front for me," August said.

It didn't take long for them to get on the road. Thankfully, Margo liked riding in August's van, so she happily hopped in the back and made a beeline for the bed.

"Is it okay if we swing by and pick Charlotte up after we're done?" August asked.

"Absolutely. I miss the munchkin."

"Cool. Thanks."

Silence descended for a moment. Nora's mind was swirling with plans and possibilities. She realized she should reach out to Raymond; it made more sense for him to act as her attorney to deal with Sebastián Pérez. She added setting up a lunch with him to her mental checklist. The thought crossed her mind that she had a lot of meetings over food where a normal person would have just used a phone. Perhaps she had that in common with Lucca; she was more of an in-person kind of gal.

"Apartment hunting sucks." August pulled Nora from her thoughts. "It's impossible to find anything even sort of reasonable—and nowhere will let us have pets. Charlotte has her heart set on a kitten, and I'd hoped that being in one spot would make that possible."

"Charlotte needs a kitten." If Nora had her way, Charlotte would get anything she ever even thought about wanting, but August refused to let Nora spoil the child. Perhaps she'd let her get them a kitten, though. But first, they needed a home. "Do you need a pay raise? I'm positive I owe you one."

"You don't have to give me a pay raise."

Nora wasn't hearing it. "Pru wants to cut back, to focus on her art. If you want to take on some of her responsibilities, that's worth a raise."

"You just gave me a raise at my 90-day mark, remember?"

"This is different. Besides, you're a good employee. If what you make isn't a living wage, then we need to address that."

"We can fight about this later." August waved the conversation away. "I want to know if there are any updates on you and the detective."

"He has rather grown on me," Nora admitted. Maybe it was seeing how much pain August and Leo were causing themselves by not admitting their feelings for each other, but Nora was finding it harder and harder to remember why she was so insistent on keeping Rafael at bay.

They pulled into the parking lot at the lighthouse, saving Nora from having to expound on that declaration. August offered to wait in the car with Margo, so Nora hurried inside, hoping to catch Arin.

The other woman was in the middle of giving a tour, but she slipped away when she saw Nora. She fished through her bag to produce a thumb drive, pressing it into Nora's hand as she said, "I found it."

"We can talk more when you get off work, but just tell me this: is it in US or international waters?" Nora asked, barely above a whisper.

Arin replied by way of a big grin. "You are one lucky lady."

Nora closed her eyes, relief washing over her. She hadn't given it much thought until this moment, but she was worried she was planning bigger than even her budget could allow. Maybe that's why she had treasure fever so bad. Or maybe, she just liked solving mysteries, especially old ones. Still, knowing that she could keep both hauls if she found them made the allure of solving this particular mystery that much sweeter.

"Thank you," she said. "And please do swing by the house sometime this week. I'll text the address—and I'll make Rafael feed you."

"I have no idea who that is, but okay," Arin agreed before scurrying back to her tour.

Nora gripped the drive so hard that she could feel it cutting into her palm as she walked back to the van, hoping she looked calmer than she felt. She climbed in the passenger seat, and instantly grabbed her laptop, popping it open and putting the thumb drive in while a curious August watched.

It didn't take Nora long to navigate to the file Arin had left for her. It opened, revealing a series of coordinates overlaid on a nautical map that, in essence, mapped out a rectangle where Nora should begin her search. A rectangle just far enough outside the boundary line for U.S. waters to make it hard to dispute.

"Judging by the look on your face, she had good news for you."

Nora's grin deepened, if that was even possible. "She did."

"Where to next?"

Nora leaned forward and put an address in the van's GPS. "This address."

"Do I want to know where that is?"

"Probably not, no," Nora admitted.

When they pulled up to the wrought iron gate barring the entrance to a sprawling estate, August looked over at Nora. "You're right. I didn't want to know."

The box squawked at them, and a gruff-sounding man asked

them to state their business. Nora leaned over so her face would be visible to the camera and told him who she was and that she needed to speak to Lucca. The box went silent, and the women waited for a verdict. August had nearly talked herself into backing up and turning around when the gate swung open.

"Now what?" August froze.

"Now, we go see a mob boss about a boat."

CHAPTER TWELVE

Nora remembered looking over at August as they walked down the driveway to the door and wondering just what Lucca would think of her. She was wearing a lavender t-shirt that said, "Too bad being sassy doesn't burn calories" and a purple paisley broom skirt. Her red hair was blowing wild and free in the wind, and she held her key between her fingers like a weapon.

As it turned out, Lucca adored her. They'd met before in the shop, but she still somehow felt the need to curtsey to the man when he greeted them. He laughed, grabbed her upper arms, and soundly kissed each cheek. August was so startled that she dropped the keys that were meant to be her salvation if things when awry. They clattered noisily on the floor and Nora knelt to pick them up.

After greeting August, Lucca had turned to Nora, his face growing serious. "Nora, my dear, tell me how things went so sideways with Mykal."

"It was Rafael's fault," August leaned over and whispered noisily. "But you can't blame him. He's just worried about Nora."

Lucca tsked and shook his head. "You should not have taken him with you, Nora."

"Maybe," she conceded. "But it actually worked out pretty well for you. I found out that Terra doesn't hate you, and she intended for you to know Mykal."

"Really?" His eyes lit up.

Nora nodded. "She's just being cautious. She's not comfortable with your world. Give her time and I think she'll reach out."

Lucca clapped his hands together. "Wonderful. Wonderful. And Mykal?"

"Last I saw her, she was still processing the information that her father was in this city," Nora answered. "She'd never even heard your name before, but I think she's curious. She'll find a way to get in touch; I'm sure of it."

"Excellent!" He beamed at her, his earlier irritation forgotten. "We must celebrate!"

"As much as I'd love to, I have to pick up my kiddo from preschool soon," August declined.

Nora hitched her thumb toward August. "Sorry; she's my ride."

"All right, then we will talk business. I'm sure you didn't come simply to tell me about my daughter."

"I came to see if you'd be interested in getting back into the treasure game," Nora said.

"How much do you need?"

"Not money." Nora shook her head. "I need to borrow the *Magnolia Jane*."

"What happened to *Amelia*? Is she hurt?"

"*Amelia* is fine." Nora let it go that he referred to the boat as if she were a person. "But I just leased her out to a friend to film a show. I don't want to wait for him to get back, so I thought I'd see if the *Magnolia Jane* was free."

Lucca had seemed unsure initially, but it was August who won him over to the idea, teasing that he should go along to chaperone Nora and Rafael. By the time they'd left, they'd secured permission to borrow the boat for as long as they needed her.

In all, it was a successful visit, but one thing in particular stuck in Nora's mind, bothering her. As they'd been about to leave, they'd been joined by a middle-aged man in a dark gray suit. Lucca introduced him as Tony, his right-hand man. He had slicked-back hair, expensive jewelry, and a menacing face. Poor Margo pressed in closer to Nora when he joined them. Nora tried not to read too much into it—she didn't trust herself not to jump to conclusions because the man was a walking stereotype—but she didn't like the look that crossed his face when Lucca proudly announced they were treasure hunters once more.

After leaving Lucca's, they stopped by to pick Charlotte up from preschool, who was thrilled to find Nora and Margo waiting in the van when she got there. August dropped Nora back at the shop before heading out for the day. She was feeling pretty good about her afternoon of subterfuge until she waltzed through the shop door only to find Rafael leaning casually against the counter, chatting with Pru.

"You're charming, but you're still not forgiven for chasing Mykal off," Pru was telling him. "She brought us free food. Good food."

"Take her free books. Maybe it'll mend fences," he suggested.

"Free books aren't as good as free food."

"They are unless you're a total animal," Nora teased.

"Ah, there she is." Rafael tilted his head and regarded Nora. "You are a very difficult woman to protect, you know that?"

"What?" Nora feigned innocence. "I'm fine."

"Uh-huh." He wasn't buying it. "And where exactly were you and August this afternoon?"

"Taking care of things." Nora dodged the answer.

"Things, huh?" He seemed to be battling with amusement.

"If you feed me dinner, I'll tell you what things."

"How can I resist an offer like that?"

"Ugh." Pru pretended to gag. "You two are so freaking adorable; I can't even stand it. Just leave already."

Nora blushed, protesting. "I was going to help you close up."

"I got it. For real," Pru reassured her. "But I do need to come in late tomorrow if that's okay. I'm super behind on show prep and Diane wanted me to stop by the gallery."

"Absolutely, and thanks." In truth, Nora was eager to tell Rafael what she'd learned, so she took Prudence up on the offer to cut out early.

They walked most of the way to his car in silence. When Rafael spoke, his tone was teasing. "So, how was your day?"

"Good thanks, and you?" Nora intentionally missed his meaning.

"Not bad. Talk to any mob bosses?"

"I did, as a matter of fact."

"Nora, I can't protect you if you insist on meeting the man I'm trying to protect you from at the local diner."

"Actually… we went to his house," Nora admitted and cringed in anticipation of his response.

Rafael stopped short, closing his eyes and muttering in Spanish.

"He said we could borrow his boat," she continued before he could start lecturing her.

"Why are we borrowing his boat?"

"Did I mention I agreed to salvage a sunken ship for the government of Spain today?" Nora asked, knowing full well she hadn't mentioned it yet. "Oh, that reminds me, I need to talk to Raymond."

"It sounds like we do have a lot to catch up on."

"We do," she agreed. "Hey, Rafael…"

"Yes, Nora?"

"Do you know how to sail?"

"I do, why?"

"Because I don't."

He began muttering in Spanish again. Nora smiled to herself, wondering if it was time to put an ad out for more help at the shop. Now that they had customers, it wasn't a good idea to keep closing it up every time she couldn't cover a shift, and Pru seemed to be gone more and more lately. If Nora took off sailing for treasure, they'd be seriously short-staffed.

He left her to her thoughts until they reached the car, but then he insisted on a full update. Nora spilled out the story of her day as they made their way back to her house, continuing her narrative as they started dinner prep, and getting excited all over again as she pulled up the map to show Rafael.

"So, let me get this straight: You want you and I to take Lucca's boat to go look for the treasure James Byrd had been looking for—"

"In the wrong spot," Nora interrupted.

"Right. In the wrong spot. But then you want to send Leo out with your crew on your boat to go look for this treasure." He pointed at the screen.

"Exactly."

"And the Spanish government is going to pay you a quarter of whatever we recover from the one we're looking for?"

"And we're hoping they don't find out about the one my crew is looking for."

"I'm positive they are going to find out about that treasure."

"Hopefully not yet, anyway," Nora amended. "Oh, one thing I forgot to ask—does the name Tony Amato mean anything to you?"

"Aside from being Lucca's underboss, you mean?"

"No, that's it. I met him today. I don't much care for him."

"You met—" Rafael gulped in some air. "You met Tony Amato today?"

"Just for a moment, but he seemed pretty interested in the treasure."

"Please, please be careful around that man," Rafael begged. "Better yet, stay completely away from him."

"Gladly." She even meant it this time. He gave her a look that said he didn't believe it for a second and she couldn't help laughing.

"You laugh, but you're going to be the death of me. I think I found a gray hair this morning."

"Aw, I bet you're gonna look good all salt n' pepper," she teased.

He waggled his eyebrows at her. "You think?"

"Absolutely. You know what, Detective Medero?"

"What's that?" he asked as he held a wooden spoon toward her, motioning for her to taste the lemon cream sauce he'd been stirring.

Nora obliged, reassuring him it was heavenly before finishing her thought. "We talk an awful lot about me and what's going on in my world. Tell me something about your world."

"Oh, I don't know," he hedged. "I think my world is too terrifying for pleasant dinner conversation."

"More terrifying than creepy mafia underbosses?"

"Don't remind me about him."

"Did something truly gruesome happen at work today? Was it a murder? Do you need help solving the case?"

"It was not a murder… okay, well, actually, there was a murder, but it wasn't particularly gruesome, and I do not need help solving it. I was referring to the fact that my mother called."

"I thought you liked your mother."

"Oh, but you haven't heard what the conversation was about."

"What?" Nora leaned forward on her stool curious.

"She wants to know when she's going to meet the lovely young woman I'm dating."

Nora was crushed. "You're dating someone?"

Rafael dropped the spoon and just stared at her for a full minute.

"Oh!" Realization dawned. "She means me."

"Yes, you." He picked up the spoon and resumed stirring. "One of the ladies she plays bridge with saw us at dinner. Someone from her church saw us getting coffee the other morning. Apparently, there have been sightings of the great mythological girlfriend all over St. Augustine, and my mother is beside herself that she heard it through the grapevine."

"Oh," Nora repeated, this time deflated. Meeting his mother felt so… so… big. But when she'd invited him to tell her something from his world, of all the things he could have said, he chose this. Which made Nora think that just maybe he wanted her to meet his mom but didn't want to scare her off by asking. Given the lengths this man had gone to for her since the moment they met, meeting his mother was the least she could do for him in return. "What if you brought her by the shop one day? Maybe we could all take Margo down the street for ice cream or something."

"You don't have to do that, Nora." He turned away, fishing for her colander to strain the pasta.

"Do you want me to meet your mother?" she asked softly, handing him the colander that had been sitting right beside him on the counter.

Their fingers brushed as he went to take it from her and he stopped, his gaze meeting hers. "Yeah, I do."

"Then bring her by for ice cream."

"She's lactose intolerant."

"Okay, shaved ice."

He chuckled. "Shaved ice sounds nice."

"I don't think our pasta is al dente anymore."

He swore in Spanish again and rushed to grab their dinner off the stove. It didn't take long to plate their dinners; thankfully, he'd rescued the angel hair in time. It was all almost too pretty to eat—angel hair pasta, zesty lemon cream sauce, sauteed shrimp and veggies, and a freshly chilled glass of pinot grigio. He was so much more relaxed after she'd agreed to meet his mother that Nora couldn't help wondering if his earlier nerves had more to do with that than anything.

When dinner was over, they walked Margo and then strolled

lazily down the driveway to his Tahoe. Since they had an audience, their goodbye was brief. As he was backing down the driveway, she took some coffee over to Officer Davis.

He rewarded her with a smile. "You remembered."

"Of course!" Nora stayed to chat with him for a moment before heading back inside. It took her a little while—and two cups of her sleepy tea—before she was able to fall asleep. She couldn't say which the culprit was, treasure or Rafael's mother, both were clamoring for attention in her brain, and it took a while to get the thoughts to quiet down.

On her way to work the next morning, she swung by the new office to pick up donuts from the neighbor she hadn't angered by being deeply intrusive. Rafael had given up trying to accompany her since she'd gone straight into the lion's den as soon as he'd left her alone anyway. By the time she got to the shop, August was already there opening up. Charlotte was playing quietly in the children's corner, which had always been set up to look like something out of a storybook, but Nora kept adding to it, knowing it would make Charlotte smile.

The area was adorned with twinkle lights and greenery. The walls that weren't covered by books had been painted with murals depicting scenes from the books. A replica of hangman's tree from *Peter Pan* was wedged into a corner—that had been here since Walter owned the store. A reading tent that looked like a miniature pink castle sat dead center of the area—that was Nora's most recent addition.

When Nora and Margo arrived, Charlotte came bursting out of the tent with a delighted squeal, racing over to hug Margo first, then Nora's legs. August arrived just in time to save the donuts and offer Nora a steadying hand.

"Please tell me Leo got my text to bring the coffee."

"He did. Your oat milk latte is waiting on the counter." August paused. Her next words were spoken more carefully. "Did you, by chance, have a conversation with Leo?"

"We have conversations all the time."

"Cute."

"I did mean to apologize to you about the whole sea monster thing. I didn't mean to chew up what time you two had together."

"Well, I'm not thrilled about that, but I was more referring to how awkward he's gotten around me."

"He's always been awkward around you. And maybe he's just trying to work up the nerve to do something about it." At least, that's what Nora hoped it was. If she'd managed to bungle this as badly as she had things with Mykal, she'd be good and truly angry with herself.

Leo loped down the stairs with his usual, distinctive cadence, which Nora attributed to his uncannily long legs. He smiled and waved at Nora before sidling up to her and resting his head on her shoulder, mimicking what she'd done to him when she wanted something, only it was infinitely more amusing when he did it because he had to stoop to accomplish the pose. Looking back up at Nora required him to contort in ways she hadn't thought possible for him.

"Nora, my friend—"

Nora laughed and side-stepped away even as she shooed him off her. "You goofball. Just tell me what you want."

"It occurs to me that if you were to become an investor on the show, Casimir would be much more receptive to changing our schedule. Then I could spend the three weeks filming and still get my break here in St. Augustine to…do…other things." he fumbled over that last part, his eyes flicking to August as he did.

"Would it mean I have to interact with Casimir?" Nora asked.

"Nope. Just write the checks and I'll be the go-between."

"What's your budget shortfall?"

"It's not so much a shortfall as a limiting factor."

Nora gave him a look that said she wasn't interested in the semantics. "Get me a number and I'll take it to Ivy to see if it's feasible. But I need the *Amelia* to ship out as soon as Captain Angelou has her ready."

His grin broadened and he bounded back up the stairs, presumably to go call Casimir to get the magic number. Nora tried to call Raymond's office, but nobody answered the phone. She assumed that must mean Lissa was on her honeymoon and the temp was working out about as well as expected. She made a note to swing by after lunch to see if she could catch him. He'd probably be in court right now anyway.

They got the store opened and hours ticked by without incident, making it incredibly difficult for Nora to think about anything other than her looming date with Rafael and his mother. Pru breezed in at some point. Nora tried to visit with her, but Pru was so distracted that it was a lost cause.

Nora did manage to get Pru's attention long enough to tell both of her staff that she was hiring a third employee, someone to help cover gaps in their shifts. It was decided that Pru would place the ads and the two women would split up the interviews between them. Nora agreed to do second interviews if they found someone before she and Rafael set sail, which Nora hoped they would.

When the meeting dispersed, August went to round up Charlotte so they could grab some lunch and sunshine before Nora left to meet Rafael. She found the girl sitting curled up in her tent, hugging her knees and looking forlorn.

"Charlotte, honey, what's wrong?" August got down on all fours and crawled into the tent with her daughter. It took a few moments of prodding to get the answer out of the girl.

"Leo's going away. And now Miss Nora's going away, too."

"They won't be gone long, sweetheart. They're coming back," August promised.

Nora stood quietly by, watching the pair and unsure how to help or if it was even her place to. When her heart could take it no more, she crawled into the tent with them and held her arms out for a hug.

TROUBLE IN THE TREASURE

"Sweet Charlotte, you and your mommy are my dearest friends. I will always come back to you." Even as Nora said the words, she knew that some of the things she did were dangerous. She knew all too well that sometimes people don't come back, even if they want to. It's why she'd kept Rafael at bay for so long, and it's why she wasn't sure she'd ever want to have children of her own. Being Charlotte's adoptive auntie already had her heart walking around outside her body. She wasn't sure she could handle having that amplified by having children. Regardless, it was a conversation she knew she needed to have with Rafael before she allowed whatever they were to go any further.

Pushing all of that aside for now, she focused on the matter at hand. "Did I ever tell you the story of the dinosaur dance party?"

She could feel Charlotte shake her head.

"Oh, my goodness, that's my favorite story. I can't believe I forgot." Nora launched into a completely ridiculous tale of dinosaur friends who organized a dance party so amazing that even the T-Rex came and promised not to eat anyone. By the end of the tale, August, Nora, and Charlotte were dancing around the children's area, alternately wiggling their butts and roaring, dancing like dinosaurs do. Margo thought it was great fun and hopped up and down on her front feet, getting as close to Nora as she possibly could so she could be in on the action.

Unfortunately, Margo got a little too close, getting tangled up in Nora's legs and sending her backward, where she bumped into a shelf, which teetered dangerously into the princess tent. She twisted, trying to catch the shelf, but ultimately wound up riding the bookshelf like a surfboard on a wave of pink tent as they all came crashing down.

"Oof. Thanks for that, Margo." Nora lay face down, sprawled across the bookshelf for a moment, trying to catch her breath. Charlotte and August watched in horror. And then another pair of legs came into view and Nora looked up to see Rafael looking down on her, concern and amusement on his face.

"Are you okay?" he asked, kneeling.

"Peachy." She omitted that she might die of embarrassment.

"So, Nora, this is my mom, Camila Medero, and my abuela, Sofía González. Ladies, meet Nora."

CHAPTER THIRTEEN

NORA SQUINTED AGAINST THE SUN, TRYING TO READ THE LATEST readouts they'd received from the seafloor below. By no means an expert, she'd gotten pretty good at interpreting the data.

They were, in effect, "mowing the lawn" with a multibeam mapping system that had been mounted on the *Magnolia Jane*'s hull, using a swath of sonar to map large areas of the ocean's floor with each passing, greatly reducing the time needed to canvas an area. What would have, at one time, taken months or even years, could now be accomplished in weeks or even days—assuming Arin's math was correct, and she'd given them the right search area to begin with.

With Rafael steering and her keeping an eye on data and being his extra set of hands when needed, they sailed from one end of the search area to the other, mapping the ocean's floor below and sending the data to Arin, who would tell them when they'd found something worth taking a closer look at. As of yet, they'd yet to find something worth taking a closer look at.

It felt like a million years since Nora had made her graceful first impression on Rafael's mother and grandmother. After setting the children's area back to rights, which Rafael had insisted on helping with when she would have gladly left it that way just to be away from the mortification of the moment, they'd gone for lunch.

A sit-down meal was more than Nora remembered agreeing to, but there was no polite way to decline, so she'd gone along. And, in so doing, heard at least six times how great a disappointment it was that she was not Catholic.

Aside from that—and from feeling like a jerk for making August order lunch in because Nora skipped in line for her break—the meal had gone fairly well. Though when your first impression is the dinosaur wiggle followed by taking down half a section of a bookstore, there is nowhere to go but up.

Nora had to appreciate that Rafael not only didn't run after that disastrous day, but he had moved mountains to get off work for this little adventure of theirs. He'd also worked closely with Oliver to help get their sailboat ready while Nora worked with Raymond to get the contracts in place.

It had been a hustle to get the *Amelia* ready for her own voyage. That ship already had equipment mounted to its hull to help map the seafloor beneath, but Nora had still upgraded it. Time was of the essence here, and she didn't want to leave anything to chance.

What surprised Nora most was how easy it had been to convince Arin to quit her job at the lighthouse to go with the crew of the *Amelia*. Although, maybe it shouldn't have surprised her. If they found what they were looking for, Arin wouldn't need a job—she could fund her own expeditions for a while.

After all of the hurry and scurry and wondering what happened when you blinked and a whole week would have gone by, it was crazy to be spending their days much the same, sailing up and down the coastline. After weeks of looking over her shoulder, wondering if someone was going to jump out the shadows to steal her map, nothing. Even Officer Davis had been reassigned. Whoever had been after the maps now seemed to be content to let her track down the treasure, but maybe that's what they'd been after all along. Maybe the shadowy figures and near misses had actually been attempts to corral her, not stop her.

Nora's skin felt tight and prickly, warmed by the sun—though it had taken on a lovely golden glow of late. Sometimes, when Nora got home at night, she felt like she was still rolling on the waves. There were times when she delighted in every aspect of this, from the sound of the wind filling the sails, to the lapping of the water as their ketch slid through it, to the spray of salty air in her face. But sometimes, she wished the ground would stop moving beneath her.

Rafael, however, looked like he could do this forever and love every minute of it. He was a patient teacher, filling her in on the terms she'd need to know. He also taught her how to tie a knot—after much bickering, giggling, and debate, that is.

The *Amelia* was out in much deeper—and more dangerous—waters, so she and her crew were out to stay until her job was done. The *Magnolia Jane*, however, was searching close enough to shore that they were able to leave before dawn each morning and come back at dusk. Which is how Lucca was able to sweet-talk himself onto the boat.

He'd shown up at the marina that morning, dressed for a day of sailing, and had pleasantly informed them that it was his boat, and he wanted in on the fun.

"It's bad enough that I'm on your boat helping find treasure for a suspect Spanish organization that claims to represent the government. How's it going to look if I spend the day with you? Everyone's going to think I'm in your pocket."

"Oh, my dear boy. You would not be the first person in your department that we've purchased." Lucca patted Rafael on the shoulder and walked past him to board the boat.

Rafael had looked to Nora, who shrugged. It was Lucca's boat, after all. The first few hours had been strained, but things began to ease up as it became more apparent that Rafael now had someone else on board who knew what they were doing, making his day much easier. It also freed Nora up to pay closer attention to the equipment, giving them faster results.

Now was one of those somewhat rare but entirely lovely moments of calm, when all three of them were free to sit in the sunshine and delight in the breeze.

"I knew your father, you know," Lucca told Rafael. "He was a good man."

"Yeah, there were plenty of rumors about you and my father."

"They were just rumors." Lucca met Rafael's gaze. "He wasn't on our payroll."

Rafael swallowed, clearly emotional at the news. Nora wondered what the story was there. She supposed she could look it up, but it was better to wait and let Rafael tell her in his own time. Still, the exchange shed some light on his resistance to Lucca—and made her appreciate all the more that he was here, on Lucca's boat, because she'd asked him to be.

Not wanting to intrude on what felt like a private moment between the two, she quietly slipped away under the pretense of checking the latest readings. But when she did, it only took a second to register what she was looking at.

"Stop! How do we stop this thing?" Nora's heart was beating hard in her chest as she stared at the screen.

"What? What's wrong?" Rafael rushed toward her.

"Not wrong. Right. Look!" She pointed at the blip of colors on the screen. Their instruments used colors to mark depth, red was the shallowest, then yellows, greens, and finally blues. And there, on her screen, was a rainbow-colored shape of a boat. At least half of it, anyway.

He looked at the screen, then grinned at her, planting a noisy kiss on her forehead before looking over at Lucca.

Lucca held up a hand. "Don't even think about kissing me."

Rafael laughed. "Shut up and help me turn the boat, old man."

He might have turned the boat into the wind to stop it, but

Nora was glad it gave her a chance to scan the area again, going back the other way. Not only did it confirm her results, but it also gave her a chance to mark the exact location of their find.

After the anchor was set, Rafael went about suiting up. As the only qualified diver in the group, it was up to him to go explore the area below to see if the colorful blips on the screen were the ship they'd been looking for. As she helped him suit up, she realized how badly she wished she was going down there with him. He'd be relaying video back for them to see what he saw, but it wasn't the same.

"I think I need to find myself some scuba classes," she told him.

"I'd like that. I know exactly where I want to take you when you're certified."

"Good. It's a date."

"You mean a non-date date," he teased.

"No, I mean a date-date." She popped up on her tiptoes to give him a quick kiss on the lips. "And, you're taking at least half of my share of the profits on this little venture. I wouldn't have found it without you."

"We haven't found it yet," he reminded her.

"Then stop talking and get down there and find me a treasure." She winked.

He laughed, settling his equipment into place before slipping into the water. Nora waited to be sure he was successfully launched before coming back to the screen to watch his progress from the camera feed.

Being out on this boat, watching him explore the vastness beneath, she suddenly felt so small. For the first time, she truly had a sense of how much bigger the world was than her little bubble. There were so many mysteries to explore, there was so much to see. She wanted to take it all in and feared she'd never have time to even scratch the surface.

"Look." Lucca interrupted her thoughts. "There. That's part of the bow."

"How can you tell?" Nora peered more closely.

"The outline, there." He ran his finger along the screen to show her.

"I see it now. You're right." Excitement mounted, but she tried to keep it at bay. It was a ship, but was it the one they were looking for?

It was killing Nora not to be part of it. She wanted to be down there with him, reaching out and touching history with her own hands. The ship looked to be from the right era, but it was so badly eroded, it was hard to say. The sea had done a fine job making the wreckage its own, and it was often hard to tell what was ship and what was the natural contour of the ocean floor.

And then, a crudely shaped coin. And another. She watched with bated breath as Rafael reached out to pick up a coin, turning it over in his hand. It was hard to say without seeing it in person, but it looked like the real deal.

He held on to the coin, swimming further down the length of the ship, toward what looked to be a broken mast. There was an eerie reverence to the place. Nora realized quite suddenly that more than sunken treasure, they were in a graveyard. This was the final resting place of at least one hundred souls.

Suddenly, more than the treasure, she wanted to know their stories. She wanted their stories told. Yes, she'd signed a contract to salvage this ship for the government of Spain, but did reclaiming the silver and gold have to be mutually exclusive of preserving the artifacts and uncovering the stories they told?

Lucca chuckled and patted Nora on the back. "It would make Walter happy knowing you found the treasure with *Janey*."

"I think it would make him even happier knowing I found it with you." Nora impulsively hugged him. "We did it. I can't believe we actually found it."

"This was the fun part. Next comes the painstaking task of raising the treasure—and fighting off everyone else who's going to want a piece of it. You really do need to get the *Amelia* back here. She's much better suited for this sort of thing."

"Well, she's busy right now." Nora's thoughts went to her captain and crew. She wondered how they were faring with their search—and how Leo was doing with his sea monster. "If I need to, I'll hire another crew."

"Where do you think you can find one in a hurry, one you can trust, no less?"

"I might have some ideas." Nora didn't elaborate, mostly because at this point, they were no more than ideas. "But today, we're just going to bask in the glory of finding it."

They watched, side by side, as Rafael explored some more. When he resurfaced, the trio rejoiced together, each wearing a massive grin as they passed the coin from one to the other, turning it over and over in their hands and studying every detail.

Then, almost grudgingly, they dropped a marker buoy as a backup to the position they'd already marked on the map and sailed for home. It was a long trip, made even longer by the fact that they wanted nothing more than to be right back at the treasure, uncovering its secrets.

Nora sent a picture of the coin they'd found to Arin, who confirmed it was a Spanish real. The presence of reales made it fairly likely they'd found what they were looking for. The little trio was feeling pretty proud of themselves as they docked the boat for the day. They'd made it back before the sun sank over the horizon. Nora, for one, could not wait to see her dog and get a shower.

Still, as eager as she was to be home, she lingered on the dock with them for a moment more. There was something magic about this day and she wasn't quite ready for it to end. She could see why Walter was so hooked. Personally, she'd be glad to hand the reins over to Captain Angelou, but she wouldn't trade this one intoxicating experience for anything.

She was vaguely aware of Rafael and Lucca arguing over

who should keep the coin when, out of nowhere, Rafael wrapped his arms around Lucca with such force that it sent them both tumbling as a shot rang out. Lucca let out a cry of pain; Rafael yelled at her to get down. Even as she dropped to the ground, the thought crossed Nora's mind that she was getting really tired of being shot at.

CHAPTER FOURTEEN

Nora's hopes of a bubble bath and cool sheets evaporated as she sat in the passenger seat of Rafael's Tahoe, following the ambulance to the hospital. It had all been such a blur, but there was one thing she was certain of. She shifted her gaze over to Rafael.

"You saved Lucca Buccio's life today. You know that, right?"

"I might not like what the man does for a living, but I'm not going to let him be gunned down right in front of me."

"You're a good man, Detective Medero."

As usual, when anyone complimented him, he looked embarrassed. "I'm going to find out who did this."

"I know you will. Thanks for taking me to the hospital first. I don't think Lucca should be alone."

"What about Margo? Do you need to get her picked up?"

"August said she and Charlotte would stay the night in the guest bedroom."

"You mean the master bedroom, right?"

Nora shrugged. "I figure it's my house. I can set it up however I want."

He chuckled. "You're cute. Even if you aren't Catholic."

"Oh, my goodness, please not that again." Nora groaned and

rolled her head back. "Do you think your abuela is ever going to like me?"

"She likes you. She's still giggling over you taking out that princess tent like Godzilla in a Japanese village—and she's convinced she'll get you to convert someday—but she likes you."

Nora laughed, harder than she would have thought possible after what had just happened, but his description made her giggle and the adrenaline of the day was wearing off, and she found she was in that place where it was laugh or cry and she chose to laugh.

Rafael surprised her by parking at the hospital and insisting on helping her get to where she needed to be, saying his badge might make them more inclined to let her stay. Once she was settled, he gave her a long hug before heading back to the docks, which were now a crime scene. He'd warned her an officer might be by in a bit to take her statement.

In the meantime, she was left with nothing to do but wait. She texted August, reassuring her that they were okay and explaining why she wouldn't be home tonight. Her initial text hadn't given much insight, but then, she'd also just had a bullet whiz past her head and seen a friend get shot. Understandably, she hadn't been at her best at that moment.

Next, she texted Captain Angelou. When she'd shelled out the money to rig the *Amelia* to get cell service even out in international waters, she'd cringed a bit. Now, she felt like it was worth every penny. It was nice not having to radio in just to talk to her crew.

A couple of minutes after she sent the text, he called. "Are you okay, boss?"

"I'm fine," she assured him. "Lucca's still in surgery."

"Any idea who shot at you guys?"

"Well, we're supposedly working with the Spanish, and we had the mob with us, so I'm at a loss. The ghost of a Dutch pirate, maybe?"

"Yeah, well, you could have stumbled in the middle of a turf war or something, so be careful."

Nora wondered if Rafael had considered that this could be a family fight. Knowing him, he had. "Did Arin show you what we found?"

"She did. Looks like her coordinates were spot on for you guys. Here's hoping she's right about ours, too."

"I'm going to need a crew to actually salvage this," she told him. "I can't just spend the next year at sea."

"Yeah, I thought about that. I could pull one together for you. But you need to buy another boat."

"I suppose if you're overseeing multiple boats, that makes you more of an admiral or something."

"Or something." He chuckled.

"We have the coordinates, and we dropped a buoy, but I'd like to get a team out there as soon as possible. And I'd like Arin to recommend an archeologist for the crew. Surely there's at least one out there willing to work with us."

"I don't know. They hate you guys."

"You're one of us now, so they hate you, too," she reminded him. "And I get their concerns, but we have funding they can't get. Surely working with us is better than nothing."

"I'll talk to her about it."

"I want to know the story. I want to know what happened on those boats."

"If we find ours, we'll have the fuller picture, but I suspect Arin's theory is right. The Spanish ships were dealing with pirates and a hurricane at the same time. The one you found got away from the pirates only to be sunk by the hurricane."

"Talk about a bad day," Nora mused. "Okay. I'm going to go see if they have any updates on Lucca. I'll start trying to find us another boat after I've had some sleep. Let me know if you guys find anything."

"Will do, boss. Take care."

"You, too."

The nurses couldn't give an update on Lucca other than the fact that he was still in surgery. She wasn't family, so she wasn't allowed to know details even if they had them to give. There was nothing left to do but settle in to wait some more.

Left alone with her thoughts, she reflected on how much her life had changed since moving here. She thought about her friends, Rafael, and how grateful she was to Walter for bringing her here. She worried about Lucca, worried whoever had done this might try to come back to finish the job.

Her phone vibrated. It was a text from Leo, telling her the shoot was working out perfectly. The crews were shooting the treasure hunt but framing it as a hunt for the St. Augustine Monster. Granted, that had been a carcass discovered in 1896 that was first believed to be the remains of a giant octopus and later discovered to be whale blubber, but he'd become an expert at framing the "but what if it's not" twist.

She smiled to herself, thanking him for the update and saying she couldn't wait to see how the episode turned out.

Shortly after, a nurse came to tell her that Lucca was out of surgery and would be moved into a room soon. Once he was awake, she'd be able to see him. She texted Rafael to let him know but didn't get a response.

Just about the time she thought she'd go crazy staring at the walls, she was joined in the waiting room by Officer Davis.

"What a happy surprise!" She beamed at him. "How are you?"

He blushed at her greeting. "I'm good. Detective Medero thought you might like to see a familiar face, so he sent me to take your statement. How are you holding up?"

"Oh, I'm fine. Going stir crazy, but fine. Lucca's out of surgery. They say I can see him soon."

"That's good." He took his notepad out and sat down beside her. "Now, I need you to tell me everything you can remember about what happened."

And so, she did. Not that there was much to tell. It all

happened so quickly and was such a blur. After he was done taking her statement, the young officer sat with her a bit longer, talking to her about random things just to help her fill the time. He filled her in on his last date and asked Nora's advice for where he should take the young woman for a second date.

Not too long after Officer Davis left, a nurse came to get her, saying Lucca was awake and asking for her. Relieved, Nora followed the man back to Lucca's room.

"They tell me you've been waiting patiently for quite a while," Lucca said by way of greeting. "You didn't have to do that."

"I wasn't going to just leave you here all by yourself. Rafael would be here, too, but he's out trying to catch the bad guy."

The nurse set about unobtrusively checking Lucca's vitals.

Nora asked him if he could send a doctor in at some point so they could get an update before turning back to Lucca. "Are you okay? How do you feel?"

"Groggy. They have me too doped up to feel much pain right now," he assured her. "I do believe I owe Detective Medero my life."

"I think you're right. Do you have any idea who could have done this?" she asked.

Lucca cast his eyes toward the nurse, who got the hint and left the two of them alone. "I think I've been sent a clear signal that it's time to retire."

"Is that an option?"

"Sometimes." He shrugged. "For some. I think my men are suspicious of my newfound friendship with the good detective."

"If they could hear the two of you bicker, they wouldn't worry."

"Still, I know Tony wants my job. I'm beginning to think he took the opportunity to push me out."

"Are you still in danger, then?"

"Possibly." He seemed so utterly nonchalant about it. Nora couldn't say she'd be this calm if she was in the situation.

"Would you be in less danger if Tony was removed from the equation?" Nora asked point blank.

"Possibly."

"Then give Rafael something to go on so he can put him away. Then you retire and whoever fills the void knows to leave you alone."

Lucca smiled at her, patting her hand. "I'm not sure it's that simple, my dear. Now, you should go home and get some rest."

"I don't want to leave you alone." She shook her head. "Not until I know you're going to be okay."

"You don't need to fuss over me," he protested.

"No fuss. I'm just going to go ask for a blanket, and then I'm going to take a nap in that recliner right there." She pointed to the recliner in the corner. "Do you want some ice chips or something while I'm out there?"

While Nora was in search of a blanket and ice chips, she called and left a message with Rafael, filling him in on the conversation she'd just had with Lucca. Then she set out to find the doctor and drag her back to Lucca's room for an update.

She told them the bullet had torn through his shoulder and Lucca would most likely need physical therapy to regain full range of motion, but—barring any complications—he'd be fine. Nora thanked the doctor and mentally thanked Rafael once more. If he hadn't seen the red dot and reacted as quickly as he had, it would have been a very different outcome.

Once Nora was settled in on the recliner, she dozed off with surprising ease. She awoke to the sound of Rafael's voice reading Lucca his rights. She blinked, rubbing her eyes and sitting up straight. Her first thought was that she was glad she hadn't been needed to fend off an attempt on Lucca's life because she would have failed miserably. Her second thought was how angry she was at Rafael.

He must have been able to tell she was winding up to give him what-for because when he was done reading Lucca his rights, he walked over to Nora and offered her a hand up before whispering against her ear. "I'm going to need you to trust me, okay? I'll explain later."

Nora nodded and stood quietly rooted to her spot while Rafael went to talk to the officer who'd been placed at Lucca's door. When he popped his head back in the room, it was to see if Nora was ready for a ride home. She'd forgotten she didn't have her car here. She asked for a minute, taking Lucca's hand and looking down at him.

"I'm so sorry. I didn't know he was going to do this."

"He's just doing his job. Besides, it's not the first time someone has tried to arrest me. My attorney will be here soon. All will be well."

Nora felt somewhat conflicted inside. Lucca was, after all, a criminal. Having a soft spot for him was messing with her moral compass.

Rafael was waiting for her in the hallway. The pair walked in silence to his car. Once in, he turned to her. "It was the only way to get a policeman posted at his door. And you were right, it was a powerplay from the inside. They were going to try again."

"Oh." Nora pursed her lips, feeling slightly sheepish for not thinking of that sooner. "Thank you."

"I told you, I don't agree with what he does for a living, but I'm not going to let anyone be gunned down in cold blood right under my nose."

"So, what happens now?"

"Well, now we have a warrant out for Tony Amato's arrest because we were able to connect him to an old friend of yours—James Byrd."

Nora resisted the urge to spit and mutter a curse at the mention of the man's name. Her former captain was a misogynist and a crook who'd broken into both her home and bookshop. And he'd called her a princess. Jerk.

Rafael went on with his explanation. "We think he was working with James Byrd, trying to raise the capital to overthrow Lucca because he wanted the top spot for himself. You thwarted him in that regard, but Lucca was right—Tony used Lucca's connection with me as leverage to convince the family it was time for a shift in power."

"Do you think you'll find Tony?" Nora didn't like the thought of having an angry mafia middle-manager on the loose, looking for revenge against her because she'd gotten in the way of his evil plan.

Rafael nodded. "I do. We have him cornered in Buccio's compound. Feds are on their way. It's just a matter of time now. If we can convince Lucca to turn state's evidence against him, I think we can get him into witness protection. If not—well, honestly, that's out of my hands now."

"I get it." Nora thought for a moment. "I can think of someone he might listen to. Can we stop by Mykal's on the way home?"

"Do you think they'll see us?"

Nora shrugged. "I don't know, but it's worth a shot."

She couldn't say the expression on Mykal's face was a happy one when she looked up and saw Nora and Rafael standing in her shop, but to the woman's credit, she didn't throw them out and even called her mom up when they asked if they could speak with them both.

They listened, stone-faced, while Nora and Rafael filled them in on the events of the last fifteen or so hours. By the time they left, neither Nora nor Rafael could say what the women planned to do with the information, but at least they had tried.

By the time Rafael dropped Nora off at her house, she was so tired she could barely put one foot in front of the other. He admonished her to at least take a nap, to which she asked when he'd last slept. He smiled and said he'd call if there was news.

Nora went inside, where she was nearly bowled over by the sheer joy of Margo's greeting. The dog writhed and leaped and danced around Nora, eventually settling down enough to get a great big hug from her person.

"Hey! There you are!" August called from the kitchen. "I made French toast and bacon. Want some?"

"I would love some." Nora followed her nose, her stomach rumbling loudly in response.

August handed her a plate. "Eat up. But tell me everything while you do. I'm dying for an update."

"I will, but first—have you considered just moving in here with me until you find the right place?"

"I can't just crash with you."

"It's not crashing. It's being a roommate. And I happen to know your roommate would love having a k-i-t-t-e-n around." Nora spelled out the word just in case Charlotte was in earshot.

August narrowed her eyes and folded her arms across her chest. "I'll think about it."

"Do." Nora sat hopped up on a stool, eyeing her plate greedily. The first bite was utter heaven, a perfect balance of cinnamon and maple syrupy goodness. She sighed, savoring the simple comfort of good food for a moment before diving into the story of everything that had happened since they'd spoken last. At some point during the story, Charlotte joined them for breakfast, which made the telling a little harder because Nora kept having to pause to think of euphemisms for things like "witness protection" but she still managed to get the point across.

When she was done—with the food and the story—she was full, and she was tired. She loaded her plate in the dishwasher, thanked August for breakfast, and kissed Charlotte on the head before going straight to her room to collapse.

Nora couldn't say for sure what time it was when she became aware of her phone's insistent buzzing. She expected it to be Rafael on the other end, but it wasn't. It was Gregory.

"Nora, that bloody brilliant scientist of yours did it."

In her sleep-induced haze, her first thought was that Gregory wasn't British, so his choice of words amused her. But then she realized what he meant and suddenly she didn't care so much about word choice. She sat up straight in bed. "You found it?"

"Them, Nora. We found *them*."

"What? Where? Tell me everything."

"They're not a mile apart, smack in the middle of the grid she gave us. The Dutchman's ship and the Spanish ship. Both torn to bits. She can't tell yet if it was the storm or if they did it to each other, but they're here, and they strung gold bars and jewels for miles."

"You're kidding." Nora tried to process what he was telling her. Sure, she'd sent them to find the ships, but she hadn't fully wrapped her brain around what it would mean if they did.

"I am most definitely not kidding. We've got divers going down in teams around the clock, but it's going to take a while to sort all of this out."

Nora thanked him profusely and hung up the phone. Staring at nothing, too numb to even begin to know what to do next. It was surreal.

It occurred to her to tell Rafael. When she picked the phone back up, she saw she'd missed a text from him. "I know I said I'd call, but you need sleep. We got him and Lucca agreed to testify. It's over. You're safe. Dinner tonight?"

Nora replied. "Sure, I'm buying," and dropped her phone back on the bed, grinning like a fool. Two of the biggest events of her life and she'd just slept through them. Maybe she was so tired she was delirious, but that amused her. She laughed so hard her sides hurt. Margo jumped on the bed to be sure she was okay. Upon realizing her person was happy and not injured, she got a case of the crazies and started zipping around the room while Nora continued giggling. It was a proper celebration for accidentally taking down a mob boss wannabe the same day you found sunken treasure.

CHAPTER FIFTEEN

"What is this?" Sebastián Pérez stood in Nora's office on King Street, holding his phone out at Nora and looking more ruffled than she would have thought possible.

She answered slowly just in case he was having a mental break and needed the extra time to process. "That's a phone."

He glowered at her. "Do not be coy with me. You know I am referring to the article on the phone."

"Article?" She knit her brow in confusion. "Oh, that article. Did my team forget to run it by your team before they submitted the press release? I'll have to get on them about that."

"You are in breach of contract."

"Oh, but my quite talented attorney assures me I am not. I'm still recovering the wreckage and its contents for you, as agreed. I've merely signed over my percentage of the assets recovered to an archeological foundation that will ensure at least some of the find will end up where it belongs—in museums."

"And how will it look if we do not do the same?"

Nora made a face. "Gosh. That might look bad if you don't give at least some of it to your museums. But I'm sure you'll figure something out."

"And what of this other find? Am I to assume you will be

equally sharing that with the government of Spain, as previously arranged?"

"Oh, you mean the wreckage found in international waters, where the Sunken Military Craft Act doesn't apply? I mean, not that it would anyway because most of the treasure is strung across the ocean floor between the two ships, so it could just as easily have come from Adrian Clavar's ship, and we're having a hard time telling who the Dutchman was working for: maybe himself, maybe it was the English. Both the Dutch and the English were pretty upset when Spain gave the throne to France, if I recall. At any rate, pretty much any which way you look at it, it's a Law of Finds situation there."

"I do not believe you wish to make enemies of us."

"Oh, I most certainly do not because I have a pretty good idea who you really are. But the other nice thing about that press release is that it's turned the whole world's attention to us and our little find. So, if something should happen to me—or to any of my friends—you know who the whole world is going to look to for answers?"

Sebastián narrowed his eyes. Nora got the impression he was weighing his next words. Whatever he'd wanted to say, she was positive they weren't the words he finally decided on.

"A good day to you, Miss Jones." He bowed slightly before turning on his heel and marching out of her office.

"I don't think the Spanish government likes you very much," Ivy commented casually once they were alone.

"That's a shame, too, because I hear it's a lovely country," Nora replied, looking back down at her computer screen. She had a mountain of paperwork to get through and she had a three o'clock appointment at the bookshop.

It had been three weeks since they'd found the *Francisca* and her sister ship, an incredibly busy three weeks. After much scrambling, crews were in place to recover both wreckage sites, each with a team of archeologists there to help process artifacts as they were brought up.

Coordinating it all had been a ginormous headache. As grand of an adventure as this had been, she was inclined to take Gregory Angelou up on his offer and sell him the *Amelia* when they were done with this recovery. Of course, that would take years.

She was, however, ready to get back out there and properly learn how to sail the *Magnolia Jane* now that it was apparently hers. A week ago, Raymond had strolled into her office and announced that the transfer to Lucca Buccio had never gone through, and it had been her boat all along. Nora highly doubted that, but she imagined the story was the result of Lucca's maneuvering to keep his "*Janey*" off a government auction website.

She wished she could see Lucca, could thank him and tell him all about just how big of a treasure they'd found together, but he was safely tucked away in a witness protection program somewhere. She hoped that if her uncle Walter was somehow looking down on them, he was happy with how it had all turned out.

Nora got a little further into Ivy's mind-numbing reports before her alarm pinged, saving her. "Sorry, Ivy. I have to run."

Ivy dropped her pen and gave Nora a look of irritation. "I need your thoughts on those reports."

"But I have that interview over at the shop."

"Then after the interview."

"But after the interview, I have a date," Nora argued.

"You know I can't say no when you pull the date card. You and Rafael are so danged cute together. Tomorrow, then, and I mean it. And we still have to select the next Hummingbird recipient."

Nora brightened. "Yes. Definitely. Let's do that tomorrow."

"And the reports."

"Fine." Nora deflated. "And the reports."

"You know, I don't think Bill Gates' finance person has this kind of trouble getting him to talk about his money."

Nora held up a hand as if to stop that train of thought right in its tracks. "I am way more fun to work for than Bill Gates."

"How do you know? Do you know the man?"

"True. He could be a walking amusement park for all I know."

Ivy rolled her eyes, chuckling. "Very funny. Didn't you have an interview to get to?"

"Oh, right. Come on, Margo." Nora snapped a leash on the dog's sparkly pink collar and the pair were off.

They were only a couple of minutes late. Nora was amused to note that August had worn a t-shirt that said, "My job is top secret. Even I don't know what I'm doing."

She was making small talk with the interviewee, an older man with a shock of white hair, a cardigan sweater that seemed woefully out of place in Florida, and glasses perched on the end of his nose. Nora wasn't sure what she pictured when August told her she had the perfect person and begged Nora to meet with him, but this wasn't it.

Still, the more she talked, the more certain she was that Reginald McAfee was, indeed, the perfect person for the job. A retired English professor, he missed being around books. He was well-read, personable, and happy with part-time hours in the afternoon.

They hired him and, as it turned out, not a moment too soon. When Nora went back to the office to ask Pru to dig up new hire paperwork before he started later that week, it was to find the tiny blonde looking pensive.

"I have something to tell you."

"Okay." Nora sat down, not sure she'd like what was coming next.

"But first I want you to know how utterly amazing you've been to me. I won't ever be able to repay you—" Pru stopped mid-sentence, gathering her emotions.

"Are you trying to tell me that you're leaving us?" Nora asked gently.

Pru's gaze flew to Nora's. "How did you know?"

"You've done an amazing job here. I couldn't have turned this place around without you. But it's pretty obvious your heart is in your paintings. That's where you belong."

"Diane offered me a job at the museum. It's my dream job. I don't want to leave you guys, but... I feel like I have to take this next step, you know?"

"I absolutely know that feeling." Nora remembered what it was like stepping out of the safety of her known world to move across the country to Florida. "Sometimes a door opens, and you just know you're supposed to walk through. It's okay. And hey, maybe you'll be welcomed back at Mykal's after word gets around that you don't work here anymore."

"That is a bonus," Pru teased before growing serious. "She's still mad, huh?"

"I think it's less about being mad and more about just needing some space. Rafael and I overstepped pretty big there."

Pru looked like she wanted to defend their actions, but Nora waved it off. "It's okay. It will pass. So, when is your last day?"

They talked for a bit about what work would need to be transitioned over the next couple of weeks. The conversation ended with a hug. Nora was genuinely happy for her friend. She was mildly concerned Pru would get overstimulated in a busy art gallery with her chromesthesia, but she respected the need to try to live a normal life.

On her way out the door, Nora broke the news to August that she couldn't take the help wanted sign down just yet. She could, however, consider herself officially promoted to manager.

Nora stopped to pick Charlotte up from school, taking her to get some shaved ice on the way home. They were greeted at the door by a tiny ball of fur that was highly irritated at being left alone all day. Cleo was a ragdoll kitten with patches of brown and white on her coat and bright blue eyes. The breeder had told Nora the official coloring, but it went in one ear and out the other. She'd been too enraptured with the little ball of fluff to pay attention to words.

"Margo, remember your manners," Nora cautioned the dog, more out of habit than necessity. The pair was never left unattended just in case Margo's urges as a sighthound overtook her manners, but so far, the dog seemed to dote on her tiny new friend. Together, the four of them went upstairs to begin the arduous process of choosing an outfit for Nora to wear on her date with Rafael.

When August got home from work, it was to find Charlotte and Nora sitting side-by-side putting on makeup in the mirror while Cleo watched from her perch on the vanity and Margo looked on from the center of the bed.

August bit her lip trying to keep from smiling when the pair of them turned to say hello.

"Do you like my makeup, Mommy?"

"It's beautiful, baby."

Nora appreciated August's ability to utter the sentence with a straight face. Charlotte had been liberal with her application on the eye shadow and lipstick.

The doorbell rang, sending Margo off the bed like a shot. August scooped the kitten up and made kissy faces at it as she ushered her daughter downstairs to go help answer the door.

Nora smiled, pausing for a moment to think about how happy it made her that August had agreed to move in with her until they found a place of their own. Personally, Nora didn't think it would be too terribly long until Leo was dropping on one knee and stealing the pair away. He'd gotten back from filming on the *Amelia* and had gone straight to the bookshop, walking in and sweeping August into his arms before leaning her back in a kiss worthy of cinema greatness.

After a brief moment of shock, everyone in line to pay for their book had burst out in a round of applause. The couple had been inseparable ever since. In fact, they'd probably make use of Nora's night out to have a night in.

When Nora descended the stairs, it was to find Rafael playing with the kitten and listening to Charlotte tell him all about Nora running a red light on their way home.

"Snitches get stitches," Nora told the girl, tickling her side playfully on the way by.

"Wow. That's what you're teaching her?" Rafael feigned shock. "Just wow."

"I can't help it. I spent too much time with a mob boss," Nora informed him saucily.

"Speaking of which," Rafael lowered his voice. "I heard he's doing well."

"Yeah?" It warmed Nora's heart to hear that. She knew that's all she was going to get, but it was enough.

It took a couple of minutes to extract themselves from Charlotte and the animals, but August arrived to help with the process, so they eventually broke free.

"Behave," August called out as she closed the door behind them.

"So, where are you taking me tonight, Detective Medero?"

"Are you ever going to stop calling me that?" he asked as he opened her door for her.

She paused, placing her hand on his. "You do know it's a term of endearment at this point, right?"

"Does that mean I can tell my abuela we're officially dating?"

"Are you asking if we're going steady?" she teased.

He smiled, taking on her teasing tone. "Yes, I'm asking if we're going steady."

Nora tapped her chin, pretending to mull it over. "I suppose, but I'm not converting to Catholicism."

"You can protest all you want, but you know she's going to wear you down." He laughed even as he issued the warning. They continued to bicker as he closed her door for her and rounded the car to climb in.

"Have you decided what you're going to do next, now that you're a world-famous treasure hunter?" he asked once they were on the road. "Are you and Arin going to find some other famous shipwreck or something?"

"Oh, no." She was quick with her response. "I've learned my lesson. There's nothing but trouble in the treasure hunting business. I'm going to lead a nice, quiet life from here on out."

"Nora Jones, there might be trouble in the treasure, but I've noticed it tends to follow you, too." He laughed. "You couldn't lead a nice, quiet life if you tried."

The End

AUTHOR'S NOTE

I had a word count in my head as I set out to write this book, one that would keep it a short, fast read but put it solidly in novel territory. As I neared the end of the book, it became apparent to me that, while the book would eek into novel territory, it wouldn't make the word count I'd envisioned.

But here's the thing: As painful as it was to pull this story out of my brain, I'm happy with it. It's the story I wanted to tell. Any loose ends are intentional, setting the stage for book three, *Gator in the Gallery*, coming January 4, 2022.

Maybe that's not fair to those of you buying the books as they come out, not waiting for the boxed set, but I guess that's kind of like watching episodes as they're released, and not saving up to binge them all at once.

The truth is, it's hard for me to concentrate these days. Not just on writing, but the same holds true with reading or even long conversations. I think it's a mix of Covid brain and the effects of the pandemic wearing on.

I hear that from others, too. That they're glad the books are short because they have trouble concentrating on something longer. I created this series specifically for this time. It's lighthearted, fun, and an escape because I need that right now. The

AUTHOR'S NOTE

world needs that right now. I filled this series up to the brim with kindness and warmth and laughter because those are things that we're all craving at the moment.

So, I apologize to my readers who love a good, long story. I've decided to lean into it with this series. If they want to be short books, I'm going to let them.

I do know there will be two spin-off series springing from this one. I can't say if they'll be this size or more along the lines of my other books (which are by no means *War and Peace*—I didn't have much of an attention span pre-Covid, either). I guess I'll let them decide that when the time comes.

This book had me absolutely pulling my hair out trying to make it all work. Putting together all of the pieces of this mystery was much, much harder than I anticipated. I can't even tell you how many hours I spent researching pirates and secret societies. But, gosh, it makes me happy. I re-read it and I smile. (Is it okay to admit that?) Either way, I hope it made you smile, too.

Also, for those who care about the "rules" of the genre, I questioned calling this one a cozy. Is cozy adventure a thing? It should be. I feel like this book fits the series more than the genre, so I appreciate you bearing with me while I break a few rules here and there. Book three will be a proper whodunit.

More than anything, thank you for being on this journey with me.

xo,
Heather

ALSO BY HEATHER HUFFMAN

Gator in the Gallery

Life couldn't be better for Nora's friend Prudence Willoughby. She's got her dream job in an art gallery, her own artwork is gaining recognition, and she's got an eclectic group of friends that don't mind when she goes into hermit-mode.

So, it's understandable when she wants to pretend that she doesn't notice the weird things happening at work, like art going missing and her boss acting like nothing happened. But when she shows up to find a live alligator in the gallery, it's too much to ignore.

Fortunately, she's got a group of friends that love sticking their noses where they don't belong, and the crew sets out to help her solve the mystery. It sends them on a journey full of twists and turns, leading through the dark underbelly of the art world.

Can they find out who put the gator in the gallery—and why—before the warning turns into something more dire?

Gator in the Gallery is the third installment in the lighthearted and fun Nora Jones Mysteries, full of endearing characters, intriguing mysteries, and a dash of romance.

Don't Miss Book Three of the Nora Jones Mysteries, available January 4, 2022!

Tails, California

When you have nothing left to lose, sometimes the best thing you can do is flip a coin. Escape to Lakeport in this lighthearted romance that's the first in a sister-series to the Nora Jones Mysteries.

Elusive Magic

Some might call it a midlife crisis, but Josie Novak prefers to think of it as a midlife awakening. In this sassy but heartfelt women's romantic fiction, Josie Novak is about to discover that being a woman might not be a fairy tale, but it is an elusive magic all its own.

The Throwaways

Surprisingly warm and funny, *The Throwaways* are twelve novels that don't shy away from the dark corners of this world but always shine the light of hope. At the core of the series is a group of strong but often unlikely heroes and heroines coming from all walks of life whose lives intertwine as they fight for justice, for love, and to leave their indelible mark on this world.

Immerse yourself in a world of suspense, laughter, and love with *The Throwaways*.

ABOUT THE AUTHOR

Heather Huffman is a multi-genre author with publications in contemporary romance, romantic suspense, women's romantic fiction, and cozy mysteries. Quirky, optimistic, and a bit of a wanderer, Huffman cares deeply about causes pertaining to social justice and women's issues and has spent the past decade working with various charities that fight poverty, empower women, and fight human trafficking. At the center of her world are her three grown sons, her Australian Shepherd, and a spoiled Mountain Cur puppy she shares entirely too many pictures of. Learn more at heatherhuffman.com.

Sign up for her newsletter and never miss a new book, giveaway, or freebie https://bit.ly/31NXwey!

Facebook: @HeatherHuffmanBooks
Instagram: @Heathers_mark
Twitter: @Heathers_mark

Made in the USA
Monee, IL
28 October 2021